RANSOMING THE CAPTIVE

Traci L. Jones

Black Rose Writing | Texas

ISBN: 978-1-68433-979-2
PUBLISHED BY BLACK ROSE WRITING
www.blackrosewriting.com

Printed in the United States of America
Suggested Retail Price (SRP) $20.95

Ransoming the Captive is printed in Book Antiqua

ACKNOWLEDGEMENTS

Writing can be a solitary endeavor. You spend a lot of time in your own head.

But, if you are one of the lucky writers when you get up from your seat, and you leave your imaginary world, you are able to return to the real world to find that you are not alone.

I am lucky because I am not alone.

To my supportive loving family- Mom, Tony, Desi, Drew, Zay, and Brookie thank you for allowing me to drift off into my little world. Tony especially, for working so hard, yet making it look effortless. Without you, I wouldn't be able to write because I'd be so busy trying to make enough money to survive.

To my brother Peter for always insisting on having a character named after him and to Regina, Moriah, and Malachi for always providing me with suggestions for names other than Peter.

To the Jones of Texas – so many of you, so much love and support. Love you all.

To my agent Amy Brewer, who took me on as a client and said, "We'll get you published." Talk about making something look effortless. Thank you, thank you, thank you.

To Black Rose Writing – I hope this is the beginning of a long-lasting relationship.

And to all those young people who have made mistakes and now think that a mistake defines who you are – find the courage to forgive yourself, find the bravery to live again.

RANSOMING
THE
CAPTIVE

CHAPTER ONE
THE END

Although the preacher asked for every head to bow and for every eye to close, Jazz Sanders kept her eyes wide open. Closed eyes meant visions and flashbacks. Better to stare at the random white thread on the man's suit in front of her and let the words bounce around her. With determined focus, Jazz glued her eyes to the string, white against the austere dark blue of the man's suit jacket, letting her mind wander. Suppressing the urge to pluck the string off the man's back, she ripped her eyes away from it and began glancing around. She felt surprised at the number of people at the church she didn't know. It felt odd to realize that there might have been some small piece of Landi's life that she wasn't a part of. She thought she knew everyone that Landi knew. She didn't like not knowing things. If there was one role in life that she performed well, it was the knowing of things. Of course, at that moment, there was a list of things she did not know. Not only about these strangers who knew Landi, but about other random facts, which she usually made a point of knowing.

One, Jazz thought to herself, I don't know what Landi is wearing. Despite more than a few phone calls, and even a half a dozen emails, Jazz had managed to ignore every one of the repeated efforts from her best friend's family to pull her into a discussion on what Landi should have on today. With each ring of the house phone and ding of her computer, Jazz calmly and deliberately deleted each attempt at communication before having to make a mad dash to the bathroom to throw up after the final keystroke.

Two, Jazz thought, mentally ticking off a finger. She didn't know what Mrs. Lewis' face looked like right now. Upon entering the church, Jazz kept her eyes trained on the floor and followed the back of her mother's shoes to their seats. When Landi's family walked in, she'd keep her eyes averted.

The other items she was clueless about appeared in rapid succession in her head: three, she didn't know how many bouquets there were. Four, or how many of her classmates were there, which would have been crucial to her under normal circumstances. Five, she didn't know how many of the people sitting in the church were believing the PG-rated version of Landi that the pastor was preaching about. Six, she didn't know whether her classmates were trying not to think of the perfect smoke rings Landi could blow with the thick smoke that came from their shared vape pen. And seven, she didn't know how many people here had been the unlucky recipients of one of Landi's eloquent but shit and damn filled rants. Landi could be a little short-tempered sometimes. Was. Landi was...

Jazz was so deep in thought, so focused on her mental list, that she missed the end of the prayer, and her mother gave a gentle pull on her skirt to bring her back to reality and back down to the pew. Settling back into her seat, she thought about the eighth thing she didn't want to know that popped into her brain. She absolutely, positively did not know what color her best friend's coffin was. If she could get through Landi's funeral without getting even a brief glimpse of that, well, then maybe, just maybe, she could make it through the rest of this day without completely and totally losing it—it being either her mind or her meager breakfast. Take your pick.

Fact number nine of what she didn't know; Jazz possessed no earthly idea how she was going to continue living without Landi by her side. Maybe if she could get through this day, then maybe she could make it through the night.

But then what? The next day? The next week? The next month, the rest of her life, without Landi? How could she do that? Without being able to tell Landi, she was sorry. Without Landi being around to accept her apology. Without Landi's forgiveness, how could she make it even another minute? Another second without that?

Tears, hot and fast, started rolling down her cheeks.

As the funeral ended, another thought came to Jazz, unbidden and most definitely unwanted. One clear, concise fact that only she knew. Today's funeral was happening because she, Jazz Lynn Sanders, had been behind the wheel. It was her driving that killed her very best, closest friend, Landi Renee Lewis.

Of that one key fact, Jazz was dead certain.

· ·

After the funeral, Jazz sat in the car, waiting for her parents to finish talking. She stared out of the window from the backseat, watching her classmates huddle in groups while automatically noting who'd shown up and who was standing with whom. A brief search of her emotions regarding the groupings of friends and acquaintances resulted in surprising news: she didn't care. She wanted to be thrilled that there were seniors there, as well as most of her junior classmates, but even as she watched Brandon McGee, her long-time crush, stroll over to talk with the rest of the basketball team members, there was no spark of interest. No usual thrill of, well, anything. She noted only that their letter jackets were covering white dress shirts and ties. Normally, that would have impressed her—an event that brought out not only all the star athletes at their school but an occasion important enough to cause them to abandon their standard oversized jeans and t-shirts? Big news. Instead, the sight of the entire McNair High basketball team, huddled together and standing awkwardly with none of the usual pushing, punching, and laughing, made her mentally shrugged.

Unprecedented. Her lack of caring was unusual.

Under normal circumstances, a momentous event such as this would have caused Jazz to rifle hurriedly through her huge purse, dig for her phone so she could text Landi and give her a blow-by-blow description. Along with the required video proof. She automatically reached for her phone before remembering she didn't have it. A sudden image of her phone lying on the floor in the backseat of her car, two hands reaching for it, popped into her head. Immediately, her heartbeat sped up, and tears burned her eyes.

Don't cry, don't cry. Don't even think about it. Hold yourself fucking together, Jazz!

Forcing her mind away from the image, she glanced back out the window at Brandon. Any other time, she would have taken advantage of the fact that he was there without his girlfriend. Jazz would have casually figured out a way to plant herself as close to him as possible. Normally, she and Brandon would shamelessly flirt with each other, then Jazz would dissect each and every sentence they'd said to each other with Landi.

Normal was clearly way over. As if, since 11:31 Friday night, the usually wide-open pipeline to her emotions was shut off. Jazz turned her back towards the window and looked down at the bruises on her arms. She poked them. They were still sore to the touch. It was the only way she knew that she could, at least physically, still feel pain. Yet, as much as she mentally prodded her brain, she felt nothing. She felt anesthetized, like her brain and heart were suffering from an overdose of Novocain. Perhaps, mentally, she too died along the side of the road with Landi.

Huffing with impatience, Jazz turned her head towards the church to see if her parents were finished with their chatting and finally walking towards the car. Bad idea. At that moment, Landi's brothers and cousins appeared from the church carrying her coffin. Rose. The casket was a metallic rose and draped with purple irises and white tulips. Jazz stared as the six young men lifted the coffin into the waiting hearse, wincing as the driver closed the door slam with a hollow finality which instantly made her sick to her stomach.

With one hand over her mouth, she used the other to grope desperately for the car handle. Lurching out of the car, she ran to a dumpster at the edge of the church parking lot, ducked behind it, and threw up. When she was finished, she stood and wiped the sweat off her brow.

An invisible force pulled her eyes back to the hearse.

Landi's brother Linny stood, his arms akimbo, staring at her. Even from a distance, Jazz could see, could feel, the hatred in his eyes. Panicking, she ducked further behind the dumpster, eager to get out of his line of vision. She sank to the concrete and sobbed.

Minutes later, her parents found her leaning against the dumpster, exhausted from the dry heaving and crying she'd been doing for the last few minutes.

"Oh baby," her mother said softly, pulling her into a tight hug. She leaned into her mother, trying to draw some much-needed comfort. Nothing. She was dead inside. Numb from her heart to her head to her toes.

"Come on, Jazzy," her mother said. "We've gotta get into the procession line."

Her heart sank when she noticed the long line of cars that were idling, waiting for the police cars and hearse to lead the way to the cemetery.

"Mom ..." Jazz started, wanting to ask if it was possible for them not to go to the cemetery. She stopped her sentence abruptly. She didn't have the right to complain. She deserved nothing, not sympathy, and certainly not forgiveness after what she'd done. She didn't know if she would deserve kindness ever again, so she clamped her mouth together and climbed into the backseat of the car.

• •

Six hours. That was all. From beginning to end. But for Jazz, it felt like the longest day of her life. After the burial, Jazz and her parents went over to Landi's house for the repast. Somehow Jazz got through it.

Black with purple flowers. That was what Mrs. Lewis wore. Purple is... was Landi's favorite color. Mrs. Lewis sobbed when she saw Jazz and pulled her into a suffocating hug that lasted for what seemed like forever. It took all her willpower to put her arms around Mrs. Lewis. Jazz concentrated on making sure that her arms did not hang by her sides like dead weight but reached up and hugged Mrs. Lewis back. It was the least she could do. When, at last, Mrs. Lewis pulled back, Jazz made herself look into the eyes of her best friend's mother. The sadness and dismay she saw were like a punch in the stomach. That intense flash of feeling made Jazz smile a sad little smile, which Mrs. Lewis returned. It stunned her when Mrs. Lewis grabbed a tissue and gently wiped her face. She hadn't realized that she, too, was crying.

Minutes ticked by slowly, and the longer her family stayed, the more surreal the whole experience became for Jazz. It was almost as if she was watching someone play her from afar.

Look! Here is Jazz talking quietly with the principal of her high school.

"Yes, Mr. Savarise, I'm fine. I hope to return to school soon. Yes, my teachers have all reached out to me. Yes, I know all the assignments I've missed."

There she is, getting her mother a cup of punch. "Here, Mom, no, I'm not thirsty, you take it."

Oh, my! Jazz is helping tidy up the kitchen. How nice. What a caring, considerate girl she is. How well she's dealing with such tragedy.

Everyone was impressed.

Jazz could tell by their comments, from the pats she received on the back, and by the caring looks people gave her.

It was bullshit, of course. She wasn't handling anything well. Her heart was beating wildly, and a bead of sweat was making its way down her back. She needed air. She carried an armful of used paper plates and cups to the kitchen and dumped them in the trash. Then, pulling a fresh bag from the cupboard, she lined the wastebasket with the new bag and carried the full one outside to the garbage cans behind the house. With a huff of relief, Jazz stood there for a minute, her back against the garage, the full bag of trash hanging limply from her hand. Now would be a perfect time for a pull on her vape pen. Nicotine would calm her down. The buzz would have helped her ignore the compliments, the concerned looks, and the compassionate smiles everyone was giving her.

Well, not everyone. Landi's brothers had no smiles for her. No pats on the back, no gentle words. In fact, no words of any kind at all. They, at least, treated her the way she deserved to be treated—like the enormous pile of shit that she was. They weren't giving her the unwarranted sympathy and forgiveness everyone else kept forcing at her.

It hurt her heart. She loved Landi's brothers, but she knew it was nothing less than she deserved. Hanging out with Landi, Jazz used to bask in residual warmth from the love they'd all showered on Landi. They loved their little sister so much that there was more than enough love left for Jazz to soak up the remains, like the needy little only child she was.

Now, their clear disdain and disgust for her were almost comforting. So much easier to handle than everyone else's kind behavior towards her. The cloying sympathy and the unearned forgiveness made her angry with everyone, including herself.

The rational part of her mind knew everyone was relieved that she walked away with only bumps and bruises. Happy she, at least, was alive. Oh, they knew she wasn't quite her old, loud, bubbly, outgoing, center-of-the-party self, but in time, they probably thought that she would go back to being the same old Jazz Sanders she'd always been. She could tell that was what they were thinking. She knew that was what they wanted to believe. But she also knew the truth. Even if she was too much of a coward to tell them. Nothing would ever be the same again. Especially not her. Not after what she did.

•   •

That night Jazz lay in bed staring up at the glow-in-the-dark stars glued to her ceiling. She was trying to remember, if not the exact day, at least the month and year she and Landi glued them up there. Seven years ago? No. Five years ago. Sixth grade. After a science unit on the constellations, Jazz had been totally into it. She'd made Landi go to the library with her and find books on the constellations, so she could replicate them on her ceiling. Of course, as usual, Landi did most of the work at the library because Jazz was distracted when a group of boys from their middle school appeared. While Landi worked on the diagram, they would eventually place on her bedroom ceiling (the Big Dipper, Orion's belt, and the Seven Sisters); Jazz chatted up the boys and somehow convinced them they needed to take Landi and her to Dairy Queen. That was Jazz's talent—the gift of gab and persuasion and charm. Landi's gifts were, well, everything else. Yin and Yang. That's what their sixth-grade teacher began calling them.

Yin and Yang. Wow. Jazz hadn't thought about that for years.

Realizing that sleep would not be happening for her anytime soon, Jazz rolled over and switched on her light. She propped herself up on one elbow and pulled out the drawer to her nightstand. Fishing around, she finally found what she was looking for—a cheap metal necklace buried under four or so years' worth of teenage girl crap. The necklace was one-half of the Yin/Yang symbol. The black and white paint was chipped in places, but Jazz didn't care. Landi owned the other half, and unlike Jazz, she used to carry hers with her in her purse wherever they went. Her Good Luck talisman, she called it.

Jazz slipped the $3 necklace around her neck and flicked the light off. Laying back, she looked up at the stars on her ceiling and fingered the necklace before finally falling asleep.

CHAPTER TWO
THE END OF THE BEFORE

Landi had been standing next to their locker waiting for Jazz to appear after the final bell, grinning like a cat who just ate a canary.

"What?" Jazz said, hurrying over after getting a glimpse of Landi's face. That look could only mean some way juicy gossip. "Give me the intel!"

"It's over!" she singsonged when Jazz was within earshot.

Jazz grinned, couples news. There was no better way to end a day than with getting some piping hot, newly transpired couples' gossip.

"Who? Who? Wait! Don't tell me! Jamal and Aalona, right?"

Landi's smile widened. She said nothing but shook her head.

"Brooke and Gabe? Oh, wait! It's gotta be Jurnee and Isaiah, right?"

Landi threw up a dismissive hand and cackled. "Nope, nope, and nope!"

"Girl, don't make me have to beat it out of you," Jazz grabbed onto Landi's arm. "Spill it, chicka!"

Landi giggled, looked around, leaned close to Jazz, and whispered, "Brandon and LaTasha!"

"What? No shit!" Jazz screamed. "Get out!"

"No joke!"

"Don't even play like that!" Jazz whispered. "You serious?"

"As the proverbial heart attack."

"Shut up!"

Landi had giggled madly, clearly enjoying Jazz's reaction. "Girl, the boy is now officially free and available. You better hurry and make your move! Although it's my duty to warn you, he's a low-down dirty dog with girls at about every school and not worthy of your attention."

"Hey, the heart wants what the heart wants," Jazz said. Bubbles of happiness fizzled up and down her spine. She slammed the locker door closed and turned back to Landi, a huge grin on her face. "I can't believe it! Do you even know how long I've been waiting for this? God, I don't know why you hate him so much."

"Uh, yeah, I believe I do know how long," Landi answered, rolling her eyes. "And I don't hate him. I don't trust him. And neither should you. But hey, maybe you'll be the one that makes him loyal. Stranger things have happened."

CHAPTER THREE
THE BEGINNING OF AFTER

Cut, bite, chew, chew. Cut, bite, chew, chew.

Jazz thought these words to herself over and over again as she sat at the kitchen table eating the breakfast her mother had prepared for her. Usually, Jazz fended for herself in the mornings before school. But today, her mother toasted up some frozen waffles and microwaved a few slices of bacon. And now, her mother was leaning against the counter, watching her eat. Jazz knew she was being watched, and she also knew that her mother was pretending not to watch her. It was her lack of chatter that was causing her parents' concern. Usually, she was running her mouth in the morning. Today she hadn't the energy. Nothing funny or cute to say came to mind. The silence, her silence, was making them all uncomfortable.

Cut, bite, chew, chew.

Her father was doing a better job of acting like everything was normal. He only glanced at her surreptitiously from behind his laptop now and then.

Jazz searched her brain for something, anything, to say and came up with nothing. Her head, hell, her heart, felt like a big black void. No light coming in, no words, or warmth coming out. She shoved another piece of waffle in her mouth.

"Are you sure you're ready to go back?" her mother asked, breaking the silence.

Not trusting her voice, Jazz shoved a piece of bacon in her mouth, turned to her mother, and nodded.

"Well, all right," her mother replied. "I'm glad you want to go back. It'd be natural for you to want to curl up in your bed for the rest of the year. Although, that's not really how we roll. Black folk are too strong to do that. We gotta get up and get moving after a blow."

"It's pretty quick, baby girl. Do you really think you're ready?" asked her father, closing the lid of his computer with a soft bang. Jazz looked at him and nodded. He nodded back, clearly approving her answer. "Hiding from the hard ain't us, is it JZ? We are Sanders, and that's what we Sanders do, right? We power through, don't we, baby girl? We strap on our boots and get moving!"

Was she ready? Could she power through? Jazz had no idea. In fact, she strongly thought that, no, she couldn't, but the way she figured it, going to school was the better of two bad choices. Option one, stay at home. Again. She'd already missed Monday, Tuesday, and, of course, Wednesday. Begging off the rest of the week would be a pretty easy thing to do. However, Jazz knew her parents. If they thought she wasn't going back because she couldn't handle going back, then they'd want to talk about the accident. Have a family discussion. Get it all out. Figure out a "plan" to get her back on track. There'd be lectures and lists. It would be never-ending.

Ugh.

Or, even worse, they'd want to put her in therapy to help her get past it. If there was one thing that Jazz didn't want to do, it was talk about the accident, to anyone, for an hour every week until who knows when. She never wanted to talk about it ever again. It didn't matter whether the talk was free or by the hour.

Option two, go to school. The problem with option two? Jazz knew for sure that her classmates at school would be clamoring for details. They, too, would want to talk about the accident. Endlessly. She'd be the school's mini-celebrity, everyone wanting to be the first to get all the gory details. Wanting to show her the videos of the wreck from their phones. Not to mention the agony of being in class with Landi's empty seat, shouting accusations at her.

Or they'd be up in her face. Being supportive and sympathetic as hell. That would be even worse. Didn't matter whether the support or sympathy was real or fake.

In short, both options stunk.

But after much internal debate, Jazz finally decided that going to school was the best choice. There she could at least refuse to talk to anyone without some well-meaning adult thinking that she needed therapy. Blowing off her classmates' comments and questions would be a piece of cake compared to the interrogation her parents could inflict on her. The counseling brochures the police gave her parents that night were still stacked neatly on the family desk in the kitchen. A reminder that if she didn't pretend that she was okay, she'd be carted off to therapy. Something she desperately wanted to avoid.

Jazz choked down the last bite of the waffle and glanced at the clock.

"Oh! I better get going," she said as chirpily as she could manage, and for an instant, life actually felt normal. First breakfast and then off to school. She went to grab her keys off the counter and then froze.

"Oh God," she whispered.

Her car. For that one brief, shiny second, everything seemed all typical and ordinary. Then, bam! Like a lightning bolt coming out of nowhere, reality stepped in, slapped her upside the head, and she remembered. Her car. The last time she had seen it, the red 2012 Honda was facing the wrong way on a back-country road, with the windshield completely gone and the airbags hanging limply from the steering wheel and dashboard.

Her waffles and bacon roiled ominously in her stomach. A wave of nausea cascaded over her like an icy wave. Sweat beads burst on her forehead like liquid popcorn.

Keep it together. Keep it together. Keep it together.

A buzz started in Jazz's head, causing a strange sort of headache as those words ricocheted around her mind. A wave of irritation washed over her as she wished again that Landi hadn't talked her into giving up vaping. She could use a nice pull right now. Of course, they kept the pen hidden in her car, so even if she hadn't agreed to quit vaping, there'd still have no way of getting her nicotine fix.

Mentally shaking herself, ignoring the desire for nicotine, Jazz turned back to her parents. She forced her lips to form a weak smile.

"Could, maybe, one of you give me a ride this morning?" she asked quietly.

Her parents exchanged a glance. Her father smirked a little, and her mother smiled softly. Jazz's stomach did a flip. Her internal warning system kicked on. Something's going on. A cascade of heat flooded across her.

"Sure, honey," her father said, still smirking. Or was that a smile? "Come on." With a worried frown, Jazz followed her father to the garage. Strangely, her mother followed.

"Surprise!"

There, in her mother's usual spot, sat a brand-new car. Well, not fresh off the lot brand new, but a new car to her. Nausea washed over Jazz again, and breakfast rushed back up to the base of her throat. She swallowed the bile back down and began shaking her head quickly from side to side.

"Oh no," she whispered. She took an involuntary step away from the shiny red car. It was beautiful. Too nice. Especially for a bff killer like herself. "No."

Her head took on a life of its own and began moving quickly back and forth in frantic little shakes. The rest of her body ached to join the spastic vibrating of her head. Her chest tightened, then her throat. She needed to keep it together. Freaking out would cause questions and concern. And questions would either lead to necessary lies or uncomfortable truths. Concern would lead to talking about her feelings. She closed her eyes and willed herself to stop the nervous head shakes. She took deep breaths, using the technique Landi had insisted on teaching her when she'd briefly become obsessed with yoga.

"No," she repeated. It seemed to be the only word that her mind could come up with at the moment. Her heart was pounding in her chest, and she felt dizzy from the staccato beat it was playing.

Her mother came over, put an arm around her, and pulled her close. Jazz took a deep breath, inhaling a big whiff of her mother's favorite perfume, the familiar scent calming her heart down a little. She could do this. She could act normal. With a great deal of mental effort, she stopped her twitching head.

"I don't deserve..," Jazz began, her words faded away, and she waved an arm at the car. "This."

"Honey, accidents happen," her father said. He put his arms around her too, and for a moment, the three of them stood holding onto each other.

Jazz winced at his words. Accidents. Can what happened on Friday be called an accident? That would mean that the crash was no one's fault. Accident. As if it was all a twist of fate. A bit of rotten luck. That's not what happened, though. The accident was her fault. She should tell them now. They had a right to know what really happened–while there was time to return this car. She didn't deserve this, or anything else, good in life. Not anymore. This car was tangible evidence of her parents' forgiveness for her actions. Forgiveness she didn't and never would deserve.

"Believe me, sweetie, we thought long and hard about this," her father explained, gesturing to the car. "It was by no means an easy or quick decision."

"Is it too late to return it?" Jazz whispered, taking another step back from the car.

"Baby girl," her mother began softly. "We know how scary driving again will be. But you have to get back on that horse."

"This is scary for us too, you know," added her father. "Seeing what that car looked like Friday night, and then with Landi... Well, as frightening as driving is for you, it's three times as terrifying for us to be letting you drive again. Hell, I'd spend the rest of my life chauffeuring you around if I listened to my heart. But the best way for us to help you is to force you to be the independent girl you've always been. As much as we want to coddle you, we have to push you past your fears. If we coddle you, if we baby you, then the harder it will be for you to embrace life again. Pushing you is hard, but it's our job."

Her mother nodded. "We have to listen to our heads. Even if our hearts are telling us to hold you tight and hold you close. You can't be afraid of living life. This has been awful. Heartbreakingly, unbearably awful; nevertheless, life goes on."

Not for Landi. She didn't say it aloud, though. There was no need.

"You can't hide from it. You need to learn how to continue living," her father said, reaching into his pocket. "You can't give up on things, especially those things that are life skills. So, here are the keys. Drive safely, work hard in school, and have a good day."

"We love you," her mother said, giving her one last squeeze and then a gentle push toward the car.

Face your fears. Never say quit. Suck it up, buttercup. These were both practically the family motto. She'd learned by 10 years old that once she signed on for something, she'd be in it for the duration. No quitting ballet, even though it'd been painfully obvious that she possessed not an iota of grace. Give up violin before the end-of-year concert? No way, even though she'd seen both of her parents' wince when she was practicing. Allow her a break from driving after causing the death of her best friend? Apparently not. Other parents maybe. Landi's parents would have babied her forever after something like this. Her parents? Coddle her? Not a chance. There's no time for weakness with African American parents. The world is too hard on black kids for sentimental softness. Softness won't make you successful. Softness is for the weak-minded: for the white girls who live in Mcmansions in the suburbs, not the Black girls who live in the city.

Jazz walked slowly toward the car, tossed her backpack into the back seat, and climbed in. The new car smell made her want to sneeze. Clamping her mouth shut, she slammed the door, plastered a smile on her face, waved at her parents, and backed slowly and carefully out of the garage.

CHAPTER FOUR
WHEN OLD HABITS DIE

Even though she drove at five miles under the speed limit, Jazz found she was holding her breath and gripping the steering wheel so hard that at the first red light, she sat shaking her hands to relieve the pain. She could blame her jerky braking on it being the first time in a new car, but she knew the truth was that she was slamming on the brakes whenever she caught sight of something, anything, in her peripheral vision. At the end of the block, she waited so long to turn onto the street that the car behind her honked at her. Gritting her teeth, she turned, her heart racing even though the nearest car was at least three blocks away. Rather than speed up to beat the yellow light, she slowed down, her head pounding in rhythm to her racing heartbeat. In short, she was driving nothing like she used to.

A new car? So apparently, she'd been in such a fog for the past few days that her parents managed to sneak a car past her. Knowing what her parents were up to, she could have mentally prepared herself for it. She wanted to kick herself. She should have known they would do something like this. Her parents were big on surprises. They loved them, but they sucked at them. She couldn't remember the last time she hadn't caught them trying to surprise her. They both owned a couple of lousy poker faces, and neither could keep a secret.

She tried to think about all the different things she must have missed in the past few days. The signs which would have clued her in on the surprise she was now steering slowly, very slowly, down the street. Retracing the events of the last day made them clear. First, there were the phone calls to their insurance company and the gathering of the police reports that Monday morning. Not to mention the vague questions they'd asked during all the car commercials on Tuesday night when she sat staring at but not watching television with them. Thinking back, on Wednesday, she remembered her father left them at the repast. Jazz had assumed he'd ubered his way to work. When she and her mother finally got home, Jazz fled for refuge in her room and hadn't emerged until this morning. The world could have ended and Jazz, buried under her covers, tears leaking so steadily that a wet spot the size of her fist formed by her head, would not have noticed. She made a mental note that she needed to pay more attention to her surroundings. She needed to at least appear to be normal, even though she felt anything but. The pre-accident Jazz would have known something was up and would have nagged her parents until they broke down and told her every single detail about whatever surprise they were trying to cook up. In her miasma of grief, she'd missed the signs. Realizing how far from normal she was made her want to pull over and cry.

• •

Focus, focus, focus. Come to a complete stop at the sign. Look both ways. Then proceed, slowly. Slowly!

Jazz made sure she followed all the rules of the road, being even more cautious than during her driving permit stage. And because she was so focused on driving safely, she drifted into another mental haze, piloting the car through the streets without thinking about where she was going. She was driving on cruise control, so focused on how she was driving that she hadn't paid enough attention to where she was driving. Until she'd slowed to a stop. Then her breath caught, and a strangled sound came from her lips. Landi's house. She'd automatically driven not to school but directly to Landi's house to pick her up.

Fucking mental cruise control.

And now her car was stopped awkwardly, mid-turn, halfway in their driveway, her tail end hanging out in the street. She sat for a moment, staring at Landi's house through a haze of tears, numb with disbelief at her stupidity.

Shit, shit, shit.

Throwing the car into reverse, her prior intention to drive slowly and carefully instantly forgotten, she stomped on the gas. She needed to get out of there immediately, if not sooner.

"Oh God, oh God, oh God," she moaned. "Shit!"

What if Mr. or Mrs. Lewis spotted her? Or Landi's brothers? Were they still in town? Or were they headed back to college and work? Gone sadly back to living their lives, now that their one and only sister, the only daughter, the baby, the family favorite, was gone? Would they hate Jazz forever? Had any of the Lewis' seen her?

Minutes later, Jazz sat in her new car, in the school parking lot, her head on the steering wheel. Maybe this was a bad idea. Maybe she wasn't ready to go back. Maybe she should go home, call her parents, maybe... a sudden knock on her window startled her out of her frazzled thinking.

Brandon McGee.

She looked out the window at him as a flood of conflicting emotions dazed her into speechlessness. Two warring voices began to argue in her head. Jazz closed her eyes and listened to them.

Really, it's all his fault. Jazz thought bitterly.

No, it isn't. The other side of her brain replied calmly. Not really.

Please let it be his fault, begged the first voice. Otherwise, it's all my fault.

Bitch please, stop tripping, answered voice two, out of patience. It is all your fault. And you know it.

Voice one whined I don't want it to be my fault. I can't live with it being my fault. I will seriously lose it!

Voice two breathed a sad sigh before saying, Suck it up. You'll have to live with what you did to Landi forever. You're a killer. Suck it up, buttercup.

Jazz hated that second voice.

Her eyes popped open when a second knock sounded at the window. Putting his face close to the window, Brandon smiled at her and knocked a third time. Jazz sighed out loud this time and rolled down the window.

Three years. Since freshman year, she'd been dying for him to pay her more than just superficial, flirty attention. And what happens? He waits until she is unworthy of any sort of human kindness and then turns on the charm.

"Nice ride," he said.

"Thanks," she muttered in a flat tone.

Her bland, unJazz like reply threw him for a second, causing him to frown slightly in confusion. They stared at each other.

"So, uh," Brandon began again. "You planning on coming into school? Or did you only come by to show off your new ride? I'll walk in with you."

You can do this. Jazz closed her eyes for a moment. *Just pretend to be... you.* She opened her eyes and beamed a sunny smile at Brandon.

"Yep, but you are kinda blocking me, so if you could move all those hot muscles and smokin' movie star looks." She waved him back from the car.

"Oh, my bad," Brandon said more confidently, returning her smile.

It wasn't his real smile. It was the tentative smile she had been getting from everyone since the accident. One that fell directly into the same category as all the pitying looks and the vague smiles of sympathy that made her want to scream. How could she pretend she was normal if her entire school treated her like some sort of pathetic creature? A person worthy of kindness and sympathy? It would be better if they ignored her completely. Clearly, the only way to be treated as normal by everyone was for her to act normally.

"If you could please step away from my fabulous new wheels, I'd appreciate it. Give a lady some room." She grinned again, wondering if her smile reached her eyes. Hoping her voice didn't sound as phony as she felt. Brandon gave another grin, stepped back, and bowed deeply, extending an arm.

Okay, good. That was clearly a normal, Jazz-like comment, she thought with relief. Now all you have to do is act like yourself, your old self, for the next six hours. Piece of cake.

• •

Jazz pretended to listen to Brandon as they walked up the stairs into the school. Her heart pounding away in her chest. Beating so loudly that she probably couldn't have heard a word Brandon was saying even if she possessed the energy and interest to care. She felt strangely detached from her body. Well, perhaps not from her body, but from her emotions.

Entering the main hall, she could see the huddled groups of her friends.

No.

Not friends, acquaintances, and they were glancing over at her, having whispered conversations, and tapping away at their phones. She heard her name being called, and rather than go over to speak to everyone as she usually would, today, she simply waved and kept moving. With only so much energy to expend this first day back, it couldn't be wasted on these random people. Not today. B-listers, as Landi used to call them, would not make her cut today.

Brandon was still chattering away. Before the accident, she would have been chatting back. If not for Friday, she would be beyond thrilled that she no longer had to look over her shoulder for his girlfriend. Today, though, his banter felt forced. Rather than being obnoxiously playful, he was being sweet. Brandon was never sweet. Funny, loud, cocky, flirty, outrageous, charming, sure. Sweet? No.

She sighed. If no one was going to act normal around her, then how was she supposed to pretend to be?

"Here, let me hold your junk," Brandon offered sweetly as they came to a stop in front of her locker. He grabbed her backpack.

Jazz wanted to say a smart comment back to him, something cute and silly about him calling her things "her junk." Or at least calling him out on this sudden change of personality. She felt that the least she could do was give him some of the effort she was going to put forth to be normal today, but when she reached for her locker handle, her brain froze. Cute and clever words were quickly replaced with the chilling numbness of grief.

She dropped her hands to her side, staring at the locker, before turning to Brandon. His eyebrows shot up. Jazz turned back to her locker and stared at it, watching it blur as tears clouded her vision.

"So," Brandon said. "You gonna open it, or should we just go to class?"

Jazz rifled through her purse, looking for a tissue, tears coursing down her cheeks.

"Hey, you okay?"

Jazz shook her head. She turned to Brandon.

"I never bothered to learn the combination," Jazz admitted. "Landi and I shared. I let her open it all the time."

Brandon's mouth dropped open, and he mouthed, "Oh."

A fresh slew of tears caused Jazz to rummage through her purse again. She reached for her backpack.

"Thanks, Brandon. I'll carry my junk until I can go to the office and get the combination," she mumbled, her voice thick and moist.

Brandon looked at her for a moment. "We still have the same first period. I'll carry it for you."

Jazz looked up at Brandon. His face was a picture of concern, and she felt a flash of... anger. He was being nice and gentlemanly, not at all how guys her age usually were, and instead of feeling all melty and gooey about it, Jazz felt pissed off. How dare this big, hot-looking guy she's been after since freshman orientation suddenly act like she's some freaking girl who deserved courtesy, kindness, and a smoking hot boyfriend. Before the accident, he was always flirtatiously hitting on her. Lobbing the almost too lewd comments that both repulsed and attracted her to him. Well, he would when his girlfriend wasn't around. Vulgar comments she might have been able to handle. But this? This concerned sweet Brandon wasn't something she knew how to deal with. If there was anyone on the entire planet who did not deserve some fine ass guy being all nice to her, it was Jazz

Lynn Sanders. How dare he! She couldn't take it. It was too much. Seriously, what the hell? Anger roiled inside of her, even as she thought to herself that she was being irrational.

Jazz snatched her backpack out of his hands and stormed off towards first period.

"Whoa, Jazz!"

Brandon grabbed her around her waist and lifted her off her feet.

"Hey!" she protested. "Stop that. We're going to be late for class, and you know Ms. Rhone will lock us out. Jesus. Put me down. God, what the hell, Brandon? Ever heard of consent?"

Brandon set her down gently and led her out of the middle of the hallway over to the wall. From the corner of her eyes, Jazz could see the looks of her curious classmates. Great, just what she needed: more attention and drama. She slumped against the locker behind her and stared moodily at Brandon's chest.

Stupid muscles, she thought grumpily.

Brandon cupped her chin and tilted her face up towards him.

"Hey, you okay?" he asked. "What was that all about?"

"Nothing," she muttered. "I can carry my own stuff."

"No shit. I was only trying to be...."

"What?" snapped Jazz. "Nice? Polite? Sympathetic?"

"Well, yeah. I guess. Is that a problem?"

Yes! Her brain shouted.

"Look, Brandon," Jazz paused, anger giving way to frustration. Jesus, how many different emotions could she feel in the span of a minute, anyway? "I just can't. You should... I don't. Arghh!!" She pinched her lips together and frowned. How was she supposed to tell him that despite months of showing romantic interest in him, she was no longer deserving of a boyfriend? After almost an entire year of verbally sparring with him like some couple out of a romcom, how was she supposed to say that now, after the accident, being with him would seem like a reward that she earned by killing her best friend? How exactly should she phrase that?

"Look," Brandon said, leaning closer to her. "I don't even know what it must be like to be here, without, you know, without your fam. I mean, you and Landi were like them twins that are stuck together. I get it. So, if you want to talk, know that I'm here. I got your back."

Jazz couldn't even look at him. Who knew that Brandon could be so real? Not her, not that it would have prepared her from the force of emotion his words brought. She took a long, unladylike sniff and swiped away the tears. She closed her eyes, and immediately the vision of her begging Landi to go to the party last Friday popped into her head. Her insistence on them hanging with Brandon last Friday was what killed Landi. The image was enough to dry her tears and for coldness to creep into her voice.

"Let's just get to class, okay?"

Brandon's forehead furrowed in confusion. "I like you Jazz, and I'm trying to be, like, there for you and stuff. Plus, I thought you liked me."

Jazz rolled her eyes. "What's not to like? I mean," she waved her hand dismissively in his direction. The toned body, broad shoulders, full lips, white teeth, flawless brown skin. Geez, the boy even had dimples, for goodness sake. Dimples. There was no way she was worthy of a guy with dimples.

"Look at you, for goodness sakes! It's that I no longer," Jazz almost said, 'deserve.' "I no longer deserve to be with someone like you," was the sentence that almost came out of her mouth. She couldn't tell him that. He'd ask why, and then she'd have to think of some whole explanation instead of telling him the truth. And the truth was, that night, the accident happened because she was so focused on getting with Brandon McGee. Nah, not focused, obsessed with the possibility of a relationship with Brandon. Not to mention the fact that Landi never was exactly a fan of Brandon, but still was that ride or die friend, anyway. Her stomach roiled with nausea.

Bad choice of words.

And, if Jazz hadn't been so geeked over him demanding that they chase him out to a party they normally would have ignored, well, then Landi would be here right now, opening up the locker.

Ride or die, indeed.

"You no longer what?" asked Brandon. He leaned in closer to her, placing a hand against the locker on either side of her head. His face was inches away from hers.

Retreat!

Jazz ducked underneath his arm, "I am no longer interested. We can be friends, though!" And with that, Jazz took off down the hall.

CHAPTER FIVE
THE ONE LEFT BEHIND

Jazz fidgeted while Mrs. Bradley located the combination to her locker. After her meltdown before first period, she pulled herself together. As far as she could determine, she'd done a pretty decent job of acting like the old Jazz. Well, except for that whole Brandon fiasco. Thank goodness she sat nowhere near him in first period. Now, in a few short hours, she could escape from school, head home and take off her mask, and hide. Maybe under her bed. Forever.

"Here you go, sweetie," Mrs. Bradley said, handing her a sticky note. "I'm so glad you are all right." Mrs. Bradley reached over and patted her hand. "I'm sure you know there's a counselor in the clinic for the rest of the week. If you need support. Losing one student is difficult; losing two, well, that would have been just awful."

It took all of Jazz's strength not to burst into tears. She escaped the office with only a few hugs from the office staff and her combination.

Taking her time, Jazz meandered slowly through the halls to her locker. It was lunch, and the less time she was forced to spend acting normal around her peers, the better. Besides, although she was usually starving by lunchtime, today, she didn't have much of an appetite. Her stomach felt strangely empty and full at the same time.

She glanced down at the note. 47-17-47. Well, that was a combination easy enough to remember. Why hadn't she bothered to learn it before?

Landi.

That's why. After 10 years of being best friends, she and Landi had created their own sort of division of labor. Jazz didn't have to be bothered to learn something as mundane and useful as her own locker combination because they'd coordinated their schedules for maximum passing period time together.

Being useful wasn't Jazz's responsibility. She was their social coordinator. When it came to anything fun or boys or gossip, well, then Jazz was in charge. Landi's duties encompassed everything else, especially the dull but necessary matters in life, like locker combinations or homework assignments.

Based on Landi's schedule, they met at their locker before school, between second and third period, before lunch, and between seventh and eighth period. After school, that was when they would meet at their shared locker and discuss all the important news and gossip they'd gleaned during their class periods. It was Landi who decided that Jazz was best with Social Studies/History, Science, and any other class that required remembering facts. So, Jazz created the study guides for classes like that. Landi was a grammar nut, so she was, had been, responsible for correcting and polishing all papers. Both of them sucked at math. To Jazz, their locker symbolized their meeting place – the place where their strengths combined. The nexus of their friendship.

Jazz arrived at their locker, her locker, not their, and leaned against it, her mind drifting back to the last time they'd both been at the locker together, the burning of her eyes signaling that an onslaught of tears was imminent. Standing in the middle of an empty hallway, crying like a baby next to her locker, was definitely not normal Jazz Sander's behavior. She had to pull it together. Unclenching her fisted hands, she shook them out, closed her eyes briefly, and took a breath.

Be normal, be normal, be normal.

Even as these words rolled around her head, she found it so hard to stay present. Her mind kept drifting to the past. It was as if her brain was unmoored, and the tide of thoughts kept pulling it backwards. She stood there, not caring if she looked crazy, letting her mind bob around in the waves of words.

The bell rang right as Jazz felt calm enough, normal enough, to open her eyes. Willing herself out of the past and back to the present as students began pouring into the hallway, she dialed in the combination and pulled open her locker, and gasped.

Stupid, stupid, stupid, stupid!

She'd forgotten.

Hers was no ordinary locker. The locker of Jazz Sanders and Landi Lewis was a shrine to a tight friendship. The locker door was covered from top to bottom with pictures of Jazz and Landi. Homecoming, Halloween, Spirit Weeks, Christmas, pep rallies, field trips, parties, football games, basketball games, every single significant event of the past school year was documented with a picture of Jazz and Landi pasted up on the locker door. Very old school.

Not only that, Jazz was willing to bet a year's allowance that theirs was the only high school locker in the United States that smelled like a freaking' spring meadow. Landi had put enough scented candles in their locker to not only cover up the funk left by the stinky person who used their locker the year prior but more than enough to create a fragrant breeze whenever you opened the locker door. All this, and that's not even mentioning the fact that she created some sort of system for their books, so all Jazz ever did was walk up and hand Landi her crap from the last class and receive the proper textbook and spiral notebook for her next one without reaching her own hand inside at all. Granted, Landi never allowed her to get her own stuff. She could be anal about her organizational systems, but still.

Intertwined.

Had their lives been so woven together? She'd always considered them best friends, but it was only period six, and she could barely function without Landi. How was she going to function for the rest of the day? The rest of the week? The rest of her freaking life?

And she felt so alone. Sure, people were saying hi and crap, but it was clear that her classmates felt uncomfortable around her now, with no idea how to treat her. And now it was dawning on her how superficial all her other relationships were.

She and Landi created such an impenetrable bubble around themselves that there was no one she could whine to now. She glanced around the hallway. It was packed, as usual, but it was as if she'd been dropped into a teenage Noah's ark. Everyone seemed to be walking in pairs or trios. Everyone laughing and joking with each other. #squadgoals.

She turned back and looked at the color-coded notebooks, and with a shudder, stuck her head into the locker, took a deep breath, and sobbed. Her squad was gone.

• •

It took several minutes before Jazz felt calm enough to take her head out of her locker. Grabbing a pink tote bag that hung in the back of the locker, she rummaged around in it until she located the hand mirror. She looked a hot mess. Digging into the bag once more, she grabbed the emergency make-up bag that Landi made sure was stocked with the essentials and headed to the girls' bathroom to repair her tore up face.

As usual, the bathroom smelled faintly of mango and fruit-scented vape smoke. The smell gave her an itch at the back of her throat. A hit from a pen would be so calming right now. In fact, without Landi around nagging about her quitting, she could go to the gas station down from her school and score another Juul. The thought gave her a thrill until the guilt kicked in. Shit, she couldn't do that to Landi's memory. Sighing, she walked over to the sinks and splashed her face.

As she was putting on the finishing touches to her messed-up make-up, the door swung open, and the Reeves twins came in, or as Landi used to call them, Tweddledum and Tweddledummer.

"Oh my God, Jazz!" Tweedledum, aka Deborah, shrieked. "Are you all right?"

"We were so freaked out Friday night!" Tweedledummer, otherwise known as Dana, added. "We drove by and recognized your car! Girl, that moose thing was huge!"

"I can't believe that Landi is like, dead," Deborah said.

"I know!" piped in Dana. "You must be absolutely, shit, I can't even."

"It's so weird that you are walking around all unhurt and thangs," Deborah said, coming over and examining Jazz. "Oh wait, dang, that's a hell of a bruise." Deborah poked Jazz's arm.

"Ow! Jesus Deb." Jazz batted Deborah's hands away with annoyance. "I'm fine. And it was a deer. Not a moose."

"Oh, thank God! That looks hella painful, but still, I mean, you're here," Deborah said, looking Jazz over from head to toe. "And poor Landi."

"Right?" added Dana, coming to join her twin in the examination of her bruises. "It's, so, like that one old movie, you know, where death is dead set on killing certain people, and no matter what the hero does when he goes back in time to try to change the outcome, his girlfriend just keeps dying. Over and over and over and...."

"Yeah, I get it," snapped Jazz. She began shoving the make-up back in the bag because she had to get away from them. She was not a big fan of the Tweddle sisters.

"Oh. My. God!" said, Deborah. "Jazz, you don't think that maybe you escaped death, but weren't supposed to, and now that Death guy with the hook thingie is like coming for you?"

"Oh. My. God!" added Dana in the same irritating staccato manner as her sister. "Deborah, that so could be so true."

The twins' eyes widened, and they took a simultaneous step away from Jazz.

Jazz rolled her eyes. "I should be so lucky," she muttered.

She spun on her heel and walked out of the bathroom.

Unfortunately, the Tweddle twins had put a little mind worm into Jazz's head. For the rest of the day, she couldn't help but wonder that since the accident was her fault that maybe she was the person who should have died Friday night. Not Landi. Or maybe her surviving the crash, with only minor bumps and bruises, was some sort of prelude to something worse. The punishment before the real punishment. Like when your parents send you to your room to stew a while before coming in and dealing out the real discipline.

Or worse, maybe being the one to live was punishment enough.

CHAPTER SIX
THE ETERNAL DAY

Living without Landi. Going on, day by day, with the burden of guilt. Is it possible to be happy again? Does she get to be happy again?

These were the thoughts Jazz was thinking by the end of the school day – the world's longest day ever.

It had lasted forever. Years. As if this one single day had taken a full fucking week.

So unbelievingly mentally exhausting.

So, there Jazz stood, her head back in her locker, eyes closed, thanking the good Lord that she'd made it through the day without wigging out.

"Well, then again, you are standing in the middle of the hallway with your head in your locker trying not to cry, so we won't call the day a complete success," pointed out the little voice in her head.

"Shut up," Jazz said loudly into the depths of her locker.

"I haven't said anything yet!" protested a voice from behind her.

Jazz started and yanked her head out of her locker. Turning, she found Brandon standing next to her, looking at her with a funny grin on his face.

She heaved an enormous sigh. "You again?"

"You know it," Brandon answered. "So, what's so interesting in the back of that locker of yours?" He was so much taller than she was that he could easily peer over her head.

"It smells good." Jazz shrugged. "It reminds me of... it smells good."

Brandon leaned over her and stuck his head into the locker. He was so close to her that his shirt grazed her nose. She gritted her teeth as he sniffed.

"Wow. It does smell good. How d'you manage that?"

Jazz gave him a little shove back and slammed the locker shut.

"Landi did it. Bye. See you tomorrow."

She turned away from Brandon and his ridiculous chocolate hotness. She headed for the stairs, walking as quickly as she could manage without looking like she was running away from him.

"Whoa, wait up!"

Jazz shouted over her shoulder, "Can't! Gotta go!" She picked up her pace.

With a few strides of his long legs, Brandon caught her easily. "Dang. I've had to chase after ladies before, but actually running after one is a new one on me."

"I don't want you to chase me, Brandon."

"Then stop running from me, Jazz."

He smiled down at her with his damn juicy lips and pretty white teeth. Her stomach flipped. Jazz groaned in frustration and sped up again, trying to keep herself from breaking into a full-out trot.

Brandon put a hand on her shoulder and stopped her. Against her better judgment, she looked up at him and raised an eyebrow. He grinned.

"Look, I know things right now are funky and sad, and stuff. With Landi ..." he said. "I get it. You need time to grieve. That's cool. I got time. I'm in no rush."

"You've got to be kidding me," Jazz moaned, her exasperation at the absurd situation breaking her fake cool demeanor. "You just broke up with LaTasha, like two minutes ago, and now you're all into me suddenly? And what about all them other girls? How about you go get some from them and leave me in peace?"

"I know it seems all quick, but when LaTasha broke up with me, all I felt was relief. I mean, she's fine and all, but she too much dang work. And mean. Seriously, why didn't anyone tell me how mean that girl is? Anyway, all I could think about was hooking up with you. And what other girls? And does that mean that I might be able to get some from you?"

"Hooking up?" Jazz tilted her head at him and raised an eyebrow. She grabbed his phone and pulled up his Instagram with a few taps. "These girls." She scrolled through his story.

"Yeah! Wait, I mean no, I mean. Not hooking up like that. But you know, getting to know you and stuff. Like in the old days. Like they did in the 80s and stuff. Seriously, spending time hanging with you, and you know, um, stuff. Hanging out. Oh, them. They my cousins."

Jazz snorted in disbelief. "Your cousins. Yeah. Okay. You're killing me, Brandon. You are full of it. Cousins, my ass."

Jazz turned hastily and stepped into the street without looking. A car came to a screeching halt, stopping inches from hitting her.

"Dang, Jazz!" Brandon yelled, stepping in between her and the car and helping her cross the rest of the street. "You gotta be more careful. We don't want to lose you too. At least I know I certainly don't."

Jazz tried to block out his words and focused instead on looking around for the hooded death guy. Nothing. She didn't know whether to feel disappointed or relieved. She started walking hastily towards her car. Stupid student parking lot was too freaking far away.

"Anyway," Brandon continued as they entered the parking lot, keeping up with her effortlessly even though she was walking so quickly she was almost jogging. "What I'm saying is I like you. I know you like me, and I get that you can't deal with a relationship now. I'm cool with that. We can just hang out." He grinned and winked at her. "Be friends before we become lovers. And yes. True story. All them girls are my cousins. I know it sounds fake, but I'm for real. I'm the only boy cousin, and I got like ten girl cousins. True story."

Jazz's mouth dropped open, but nothing came out. There were way too many things bouncing around in her head, too many voices expressing too many opinions, for her to formulate a single coherent thought, much less an understandable, grammatically correct sentence. Especially not the usual witty Jazz-like comment his statement clearly called for. Speechlessness was a new experience for her. She didn't like it.

The only clear thought that occurred to her was how messed up this situation was. All year long, she'd been pining away for Brandon. And mostly, it was only a pipe dream, a crush she and Landi discussed, ad infinitum, without thinking that it could really come true. After all, he and LaTasha were The Couple. Both of them being blessed with movie star-like looks. Trying to look at them together was like looking at the sun. They were that hot. Of course, LaTasha was mean and petty and hard to like, but she also looked like she had stepped straight off a magazine cover, airbrushing intact. You couldn't fault a guy for putting up with her stank attitude. One look at her could make a guy forgive her for anything. Her greenish hazel eyes set in that flawless mocha face. That slim, thick shape. She was beautiful. A self-centered, nasty-tempered bitch, but gorgeous.

But now, here was Brandon, all 6'2" of brown gorgeousness, saying that he'd wait for her. Clearly, she was being punished. There was no other explanation for it. It was an absolute certainty that God was punishing Jazz for killing Landi. Either that, or he possessed one heck of a sense of humor.

• •

Brandon finally said goodbye to Jazz with a chaste little kiss on her forehead. Once she made sure he'd driven off,

Jazz put her head on her steering wheel and sat in her car for a long, long time, watching her tears make round wet dots on her jeans. She'd been saving up these tears all day long, and it was a relief to let them flow.

Still, she survived the first day back without losing it completely, but the thought of having to do it again tomorrow, not to mention for the rest of the school year, well, Jazz didn't think it was possible.

She needed someone to talk to, but definitely not one of the grief counselors she'd avoided all day long. She hated the idea of talking about her feelings with someone who would be lurking around school watching her every move all day long. And talking to her parents? So not an option.

Jazz needed someone who would tell her what to do, someone who could explain to her how exactly she was supposed to keep living day after day. How was she supposed to carry on without Landi? She needed that question answered. She wanted an explanation of why she made it through the accident with only a few bumps and bruises, while Landi had been gone for... 110 hours and counting. Maybe if she'd suffered more serious injuries, then maybe she wouldn't feel so... unworthy. That was it. Unworthy, dishonorable, and disgraceful. Why did she get to live? She was pretty certain that she'd done nothing in her 16 years of life to justify her still being here. Alive, healthy, breathing, and sitting in a brand, freaking new car, her cuts and bruises already healing. The physical pain fading.

Jazz took a deep breath, one of those breaths Landi used to call "cleansing breaths." Immediately, her nose filled with new car smell-so not helpful.

Action. That's what she needed. To take action, do something. Sitting around with her head stuck to the steering wheel wasn't going to help her not go crazy. Jazz started the car and pulled out of the parking lot. The only thought in her head was that she needed to talk to someone, and she was going to drive around until she could figure out who.

CHAPTER SEVEN
SALVATION LAYS INSIDE?

Jazz drove aimlessly for a few minutes, making random turns here and there, heading in no particular direction. She didn't know what she was looking for but figured that she'd know it when she saw it. And then there it was. The answer: St. Elizabeth Catholic church. She'd driven by it hundreds of times, and being a Baptist had never set foot inside. It was an old but pretty church that had existed in her neighborhood for almost a hundred years. While she knew of a few kids from her block who'd gone to its elementary school, she'd never in her entire life set foot in either building.

She pulled over and gazed at the ornate wooden doors. What was it about this building that made her stop? What could she find inside these doors that would make her feel better? She fiddled with the radio knob, turning it down until the song on the radio was all but mute. She needed to think, and she couldn't think with words like "grabbing my drink, while she be grabbing my dick" running around her head. Yes, the radio station blanked them out, but she still heard them in her head. So really, what was their point?

Why stop at a church rather than a Starbucks or a library? Was she searching for peace? What did the old folks always say? If you pray, don't worry. If you are worrying, pray.

Jazz looked up at the church again. Landi would tell her to close her eyes and let her chakra flow. Or something like that. Jazz would always be irritated when Landi pulled that touchy-feely yoga shit out. Still, Jazz took a deep breath, closed her eyes, and asked herself again.

A voice that sounded so much like Landi's that Jazz felt a stab of physical pain answered her mental question. "Why did you stop at a church? What are you really looking for? What do you want?"

To Jazz's surprise, a familiar voice came from deep inside and answered her.

"I want you to be alive. I want to be able to tell you I'm sorry. I want you to tell me there's no need to apologize. That it wasn't my fault. And more than anything, I need for you to tell me that even though it was my fault that it's okay. I want your forgiveness."

Jazz opened her eyes and swiped at the tears rolling hot and fast down her cheeks. She started to shift out of park but stopped. If all the movies she'd seen with Catholic churches were even halfway accurate, she might have found a place to get the answers and the forgiveness she desperately wanted. Maybe inside, she'd find those two things.

She pulled into the parking lot and headed to the church doors. Easing the door open slowly, she stepped into the quiet narthex. The scent of old hymnals and dust floated in the air, just like it did at her church, and she immediately felt calmer and less self-conscious. She walked toward the sanctuary and stuck her head through the doorway. She looked around and saw what she was searching for, a confessional box. Although there didn't seem to be anyone around, she walked over to see if maybe office hours were posted somewhere, a sign-up sheet, or something like that. Seeing nothing to give her a clue regarding the proper procedure, she felt disheartened. Frowning, she sighed and sat in the nearest pew to decide her next move. Taking solace in the stillness of the chapel. A few seconds later, a priest entered from a door at the end of the church, near the altar.

"Good afternoon!" the priest called to her, his voice carrying easily in the room's hush. "How can I help you?"

"Hello," Jazz answered. "I hoped to, you know...." She pointed to the confessional.

"Of course, certainly."

"Thank God! I really need to talk to someone. I'm about to totally lose it."

"Er, okay," the priest said, waving his hand towards the confessional. "Enter."

Jazz pulled open the door and saw a short little padded bench that faced a little window with a grate. She entered, closed the door, and sat down.

The priest looked at her through the grate and frowned a bit. "Um, you're supposed to kneel on the bench."

"Oh, yeah! That does make more sense."

Jazz rearranged her body, so she was kneeling, which took a while to do because of the lack of space in the box. After a fair amount of bumping and jostling, she knelt and faced the priest.

This felt ridiculous, and she clamped down on her urge to giggle. Landi always said that Jazz's natural default was silly. Even at the worst times, Landi said that Jazz could find the tiniest bit of humor and nonsense in anything. She'd said it as if it was one of Jazz's biggest faults. Jazz was beginning to think that it was. Some things just weren't funny.

Jazz rearranged her face, so she looked sullen and serious. They sat looking at each other for a minute.

"Oh, wait. It's my turn, right?" Jazz said, trying to remember what they did in the movies. "Okay, um, forgive me, father, for I have sin. It's been, well, never since my last visit, um, confession."

"Sinned."

"Huh?"

"Sinned. It's 'I have sinned.' 'E, D, past tense," corrected the priest. "Um, are you a member of this parish?"

"Oh, no, I go to Fairview Community Baptist, a few blocks away. Well, I mean, I go sometimes, a lot of the time though I pretend to be asleep, so my parents will go without me. Aw man, I guess that's a sin. I should say sorry for that... Or something, right? Okay, so um, forgive my father for I have sinned, um, it's been never since my last confession."

The priest sat silently for a moment. Even through the ornate grate, Jazz could see that his brow was furrowed and that he looked confused. All this looked much easier in the movies. And she was still feeling like crap.

"Isn't that right?" she asked after a moment of complete silence passed.

"Well, yes, but, to be clear, you aren't Catholic?"

"No," Jazz replied hesitantly. "Does that mean we can't talk?"

"Well, no, it doesn't, but child, wouldn't you rather talk to the pastor at your church?"

"No! That's the last thing I want!"

"Well, okay."

"So, you'll confess with me, or however you say it? Please, I really need someone to talk to who won't make me go into therapy or something."

"Of course, we are all his children. What is weighing on your mind?"

"Well, I... hold up," Jazz said, interrupting herself. "Since I'm not Catholic, does that mean that the whole, you can't go to the police and snitch doesn't apply? Like between a lawyer and client?"

"Surely, what you have to tell me isn't as serious as that!"

"It is!" Jazz cried out loudly. "Jesus, I could actually go to hell now that I think of it! Oh my God! I'm going to hell!"

"For future reference, you are supposed to whisper your confession, my child. Especially if what you have to confess is of a very personal matter. Which sounds like your confession is."

Jazz nodded. Her throat closed, and what was left of the calm feeling she experienced upon entering the church evaporated.

Maybe this wasn't such a good idea.

"Maybe this wasn't such a good idea," whispered Jazz, voicing her thoughts out loud. "It's just that I have no one to tell. The one person I told everything to is gone."

"Perhaps you'd feel more comfortable waiting for their return?"

Jazz shook her head. "She's not. She can't. She's dead. She'll never be able to listen or help, or..." Her voice trailed off, her throat thick with tears. Jazz swallowed, hoping to suppress the sob that threatened to explode from her. Her heart rate sped up, and she felt like she was going to spin out of control.

"I'm so sorry for your loss," replied the priest, his voice low and velvety with sympathy. "Clearly, you are in some mental and spiritual pain. Please, tell me what's wrong. I promise to keep it strictly confidential."

Being given permission to tell her story made Jazz's eyes fill with tears, and without warning, the words came pouring out of her.

CHAPTER EIGHT
THE LAST MINUTES OF BEFORE

"Friday night, and Landi and I decided to head out to the Wash. You know that little clearing in Gibson Woods that all the kids hang out at when there's nothing better to do. Well, it's not something we generally do. Neither of us are big drinkers. I mean, we do drink. We aren't saints or anything. But not like that. Not white girl wasted. And the Wash is all about scoring some free beer and getting drunk. So it's not usually our thing. But Brandon, Brandon is a guy I've been crushing on since freshman year. Anyway, he told me he was thinking of going there since he'd broken up with LaTasha that afternoon. Said he wanted to do something different since he was free.

I decided that meeting him at the Wash was the perfect chance for me to make a move, you know? Shoot my shot. I mean, he's too much of a snack not to get snatched up by someone else quick and in a hurry. Besides, everyone knows that the girls who always go to Wash parties get drunk and then give hea-. Oh, man, sorry, Father, but they give, um, there are girls who get drunk then, you know, go with guys into the woods, and they hook up. Well, that doesn't matter, really, but it's kind of hard to compete against girls who do that. I'm not judging them or anything. It's whatever. I mean, do you? Right?

So, anyway, Landi and I drive out there, and we wait around for a while. After, like, forever, Brandon finally shows up, and we are all having such a fun time. Landi was flirting with Ty and having a good time. Brandon and I were hanging out, having a total blast, and just as Brandon asks me to go somewhere with him that's a little more private, I notice that it's 11:11. Well, Landi's curfew is 11:30, and the Wash is at least a 15-minute drive from home. So, I gotta tell Brandon that Landi and I have to leave, 'cause her parents are crazy strict and stuff. Luckily, he asks for my snap, and I give it to him, and I drag Landi away, 'cause she is not wanting to leave Ty, but if I don't get her home, I know all hell is gonna, oh, sorry. I mean, the stuff is going to hit the fan, 'cause the Lewis' do not play with curfew and their baby girl, and they will ground her in a hot second if she's even, like, a minute late.

Even though she, like, always spends Friday night at my house, she's gotta keep her location on, and trust me, when I tell you, they check to see if she's where she's supposed to be at 11:30. The last thing I want is for her to be grounded. When she's grounded, I might as well be grounded because there's no one else I hang with, you know?

So, we run to the car, and we're laughing, you know, keykeeing it up. Feeling all happy and pleased with ourselves. Loving life. Jesus Christ were we, oh sorry, we were having such a fun time. Like the best ever. Anyway, I'm driving fast, I mean, not like 80 mph fast or anything, but at least 5 to 10 miles over the speed limit, which is kinda fast, 'cause the speed limit out on Wash Road is 35 mph, and Landi and I are talking a mile a minute and my cell phone buzzes. So, Landi grabs my phone, and she reads me the message and says it's from Brandon. This real cute message, clever and flirty. So, I tell her to answer him, and she does, and then, oh, God, he answers me back and, and, she laughs and then texts him back without telling me what his last text said, or what her answer was! And, I'm like, what? What? And she's, like, 'hold on a sec' and she's laughing and smiling, and I'm dying to know what is being said. I mean, he thinks it's me answering him, and Landi sometimes can be, I mean could be, or was, kinda rude. She had a mean streak, probably from having to deal with her brothers, plus she wasn't all that thrilled about me being with Brandon 'cause he has a bit of reputation. I don't think it's accurate, but Landi says where there's smoke, there's fire. She could be real judgy sometimes. I mean, there're some pictures on his Insta that are kind of sketchy, but so what, right?

You know what? That doesn't matter. So, I'm driving, but I'm also trying to grab the phone from her, and I accidentally knock it out of her hand. And, and, oh God, the cell phone goes flying somewhere in the back seat, and we can hear it beeping, and we're laughing. Well, I look back and see it's behind Landi's seat, so, oh Jesus, I'm reaching around behind me with my free hand for the phone, and Landi is batting my hand away, and she was laughing, and I'm yelling at her and laughing. I can't remember the last time she was laughing so hard. And then, oh, God Landi, Landi unbuckles her seatbelt and leans over the back of her seat to get the phone cause it's beeping again. I know, I should have been keeping my eye on the road, but I, I, wanted to know what was on that goddamn phone... I turn around, and I'm watching her try to reach the phone, and I'm reaching back, and pulling on her, and laughing, and then I finally look back at the road, and when I do, there are those stupid deer, those Goddamn stupid deer bounding out of the woods, leaping like fucking demons, right into the middle of the road. They're too close, and I have to slam on the brake and Landi. Landi, oh God, Landi, it's like in slow motion. She goes flying backwards out of the windshield when I hit that big stupid deer that was too slow and huge to get out of the way, and then the car somehow starts spinning, and suddenly, I'm facing the wrong direction, and the airbag is in my face. And then everything stops. My face hurts, and my shoulder hurts, and my head hurts, but otherwise, I'm okay. How can I be okay? How?

I get out of the car, and I see that God damn deer lying in the middle of the road, and it's bleeding and twitching and making this awful, moaning noise. But Landi, Landi. Oh, God! Landi is lying there. She's not moving, and she's not making a sound. She's so still and so quiet. Oh, God! I killed her! I killed the best friend in the whole world, and I can't take it. How do I live with that? How does God forgive me for that?

CHAPTER NINE
SEEK, AND YE SHALL FIND?

For a moment, the Priest sat quietly, as Jazz sobbed so loudly that she didn't think she could have heard him even if he'd spoken. It took a few minutes before she could get herself back together. Even when she did and was only sniffing quietly and wiping her nose with her soaked tissue, the priest still didn't open his mouth.

Jazz looked up at him and through the grate. She could see that his eyes were wet.

Finally, he said, "Step out of the confessional, my child."

Jazz's stomach dropped. There's no forgiveness here. And if there's no forgiveness here, then there's no forgiveness anywhere. Just as she thought. She'll never deserve to be happy again. Her legs felt like lead, but she struggled to her feet and exited the confessional.

When they were face to face, Jazz took her first good look at him. He was much younger than any of the movie priests she'd seen, which threw her. She had been hoping for an older, more fatherly-looking priest, and suddenly Jazz felt embarrassed and ashamed of what she'd told him. Immediately, her old Jazz instincts kicked in, and she employed a tried and true diversionary tactic: humor. It was always her go-to maneuver. She was starting to get why Landi hated it, but she couldn't help it.

"Aren't you too young to be a priest?" Jazz asked as she rummaged through her purse, looking for a tissue. One because her nose was gross and drippy, and two because it gave her a valid reason to not look the priest in the eye.

The priest chuckled at her question. "This is my first parish assignment. I just finished my Master of Divinity. From Duke University. Go Blue Devils!"

"Blue Devils? Really? A divinity degree from a school with Blue Devils as a mascot, eh? Geez, ironic, much?"

Feeling better but still feeling the sting of humiliation, Jazz looked up and studied his face as she blew her nose.

"You aren't bad looking. Why did you become a priest, anyway? Too shy to ask a girl out or something?"

He laughed loudly in an unpriestly manner. He stuck out his hand. "I'm Father Peter. You are?"

Jazz opened her mouth to answer but shut it quickly and looked at the priest rather suspiciously.

Father Peter smiled. "I promise not to call the authorities or any therapists. Remember? Strictly confidential."

"Jazz Sanders."

"Cool name, Jazz. Have a seat."

Jazz plopped down on the pew. She felt lighter, now that she'd finally told someone the whole truth, not the "I ran into a herd of deer" story, but the whole, this is 'how I killed my best friend' tale. And while she felt less numb, the feelings of shame still covered her like a layer of scum, and what she wanted now after her confession was a clear answer of how to go on living with this suffocating feeling of guilt and whether she should even expect forgiveness after such a major sin, and whether or not she could ever earn her way into heaven: a spiritual shower, of sorts.

With a sigh, Father Peter sat next to her on the pew, and for a moment, he sat silently while he fiddled with the beads that hung from his belt.

"Jazz, you didn't kill Landi," he said quietly.

Jazz's heart sank, and she suppressed a sigh of frustration. Even after she'd told him, in detail, what she'd done, he was trying to give her the forgiveness she didn't deserve. There was no way forgiveness for murder could be so easy.

"I can see by the look on your face you don't believe that to be true, but it is," Father Peter said. "Sometimes God does things we don't understand. He works in mysterious ways."

Jazz shifted in her seat. Platitudes, scriptures, and clichés would not keep her from going crazy with guilt or from going straight to hell, for that matter. She didn't know what she was looking for, but this wasn't it. She had a church full of folk praying for her, and she still continued to feel like crap. Prayer list or not.

"Aren't you supposed to give me some Hail Marys to say or something?" Jazz muttered sullenly. "An act or a chore, maybe?"

Father Peter smiled at her again. "Do you even know what a Hail Mary is?"

Jazz opened her mouth and then shut it again. She thought for a minute, "Um, doesn't it go something like 'Hail Mary full of Grace, something, something, smiling face?' No? Close? A really long football pass? Okay, fine, I have no clue. The movies never really make it clear."

"Well then, giving you 50 of them, or even 150, won't provide you any absolution or peace of mind, will it?"

"No, I guess no-, wait," Jazz looked over at the priest. "Absolution? Okay, so what exactly is absolution?"

"Well, I guess the quick, easy way to explain it would be the forgiveness of sin. The..."

"Hold up! That's it!"

"It's a little more complicated than...."

"Father Peter, you've given me the answer I'm looking for. Absolution! That's exactly what I need."

"Yes, but, see ..." Father Peter looked at her in surprise. He held up one finger and attempted to continue. But Jazz heard the solution she needed.

"Ok, so can you give me absolution?"

"Well, I can, but let me explain a little better. See, there needs to be not only confession of sin but works of charity and mercy for ...."

"Oh, I get it. So, I need to do something good, really, really good, and God will forgive me for killing Landi? I didn't mean to kill her. I loved her more than anyone. Like she was my sister. I did. Thank you so much. I didn't think there was any way to make up for what I've done. I knew I was going to hell. Or lose my mind. I mean, these last few days have been like hell anyway. Oh, thank you so much, Father Peter." Jazz felt a familiar zing of excitement. The one she always felt when her plans and schemes were falling into place. It was a welcome bit of normal in a day that had been surreal.

"Yes, you're welcome, but I don't think that you understand the true concept of ..." he stuttered. "You see..."

"I do, Father Peter. I need to dedicate my life to performing acts of mercy and charity. That's the only way God will forgive me."

Jazz glanced at her watch. "It's later than I thought. I better get home and start my homewo-. That's it! I can start by making dinner. This is great. I feel better already. There's actually something I can do. I didn't think I could take another minute of feeling like such crap. I felt like I wanted to die too. Thank you so much, Father."

"Whoa, wait, let me see if I can't do a better job of explaining the. .."

Jazz gave Father Peter the first real sincere smile she'd had on her face in almost a week

"No worries, Father Peter, you the real one."

Jazz gathered her things, gave Father Peter a jaunty salute, and hurried out of the church.

"Jazz, wait!" she heard him call. She gave him another happy wave and got into her car. She didn't need a whole bunch of deep theological talking. She wanted to feel better, to somehow free herself of the numbness weighing down her soul from the moment she knelt by Landi in the street.

As she drove home, never any faster than the speed limit and being sure to come to a complete and full stop at each stop sign, Jazz felt hopeful. She would have to be a better person from here on out. Not just a better person, the best person she could possibly be. Then, and only then, would she earn forgiveness for causing Landi's death. For the first time in her 16 years, Jazz's mission in life didn't include finding where and how she could have the most fun on a weekend.

CHAPTER TEN
THE END OF THE NEVER-ENDING DAY

Later that evening, Jazz sat in her room, her mind racing. She was plotting and planning, or at least trying to, but without much success. How exactly did one go about performing acts of mercy and charity? Okay, that meant giving junk away to the poor, right? Looking around her room, she took note of the abundance of clothes spilling out of her closet. As if someone pricked her with a pin, she popped up from her seat and began going through her closet. Before long there was pile of shirts, skirts, purses, shoes, jeans, and dresses ready to donate. Feeling satisfied with herself, she mentally checked off charity from her list.

Unfortunately, satisfaction didn't last long. After only a few minutes of thinking, she quickly realized that giving away a bunch of clothes she didn't wear or didn't want wasn't all that impressive—especially since it happened all the time. Her mother was notorious for sneaking into her room while she was at school and rifling through Jazz's closet, and pulling out clothes she thought Jazz didn't wear enough or were too small. Jazz would arrive home from school to find her closet half empty and what clothes were left hanging neatly in her closet. Color-coded. All she was doing now was what her mother would have done in a few weeks anyway. It was a weak effort, and she knew it. Jazz was pretty sure that donating a few bags of stuff she didn't wear wasn't going to be enough to convince the good Lord to forgive her. In fact, she knew that it was a pretty pitiful attempt at earning forgiveness, considering the gravity and seriousness of her sin. Jazz plopped back down on her bed and tried to think of something else, ignoring the sinking feeling building inside her. She could feel the soul-sucking grief creeping slowly back into her. For a few hours, it had abated, but now as she tried to figure out how to earn absolution, she could feel it encroaching on the edges of her consciousness. Mentally pushing it away, she redoubled her efforts. Something forgivenessworthy.

Mercy and charity. Charity and mercy. What exactly did that mean anyway? Maybe she should have asked Father Peter for more details before running out of there like a crazy person. Well, no matter, whole internet was at her disposal. After ten minutes of research, Jazz had a better idea of what it meant to earn absolution. In fact, there was a list of activities she was to do:

Give people stuff to eat and to drink.

Give people something to wear (check!).

Give them some place to live (not likely).

Ransom the Captive (which she guessed meant giving kidnappers money? Okay, maybe that's not really what it meant, but Jazz couldn't figure out what that one was trying to say, and that was her best guess).

Bury the dead (gross)

Visit sick people (ew).

Jazz leaned back in her chair and studied the list. There were more, but Jazz figured this was enough to start. Some of the activities weren't all that doable anyway. Even if she did have the stomach to try and bury some dead people, she doubted that it was even legal for her to do so. What was she supposed to do anyway? Apply at a cemetery to be a gravedigger? Then there was the one that didn't make any sense, 'to ransom the captive.' What the heck? Was there a lot of kidnapping back in the day or what?

As she ticked off the list of things that were undoable, the last of Jazz's optimistic feeling began to evaporate. The little bubble of hope began to shrink, and the numbness, the awfulness, the dead feeling, started to creep back in.

This was going to be way harder than she'd thought. Well, at least she'd gotten 'clothe the naked' right, even before she knew that was an act of mercy/charity. Feed people, well, that she could do. She could go and work at a soup kitchen. But would that count? Wouldn't that be more like serving the hungry rather than feeding the hungry since she wasn't the one who'd be buying and cooking the food? Should she buy the ingredients for brownies, make them and then donate homemade food instead? How many batches of brownies were enough to earn forgiveness, anyway? Two dozen, three?

Jazz sighed in frustration, wishing there was some sort of point system she could refer to. Which act of mercy and charity would give her more absolution points? Serving or feeding? Ransoming or visiting? Clearly, whoever wrote the list should have included clearer instructions. There oughta be an app, at least. As her frustration built, the tightness in her chest and throat started again. It had melted away when talking with Father Peter. But now, in the solitude of her room, looking at the computer screen, it returned.

A knock on her bedroom door interrupted her contemplation. Wiping her face (was she going to spontaneously cry for the rest of her life? Not even noticing when tears started dripping down her face?), she quickly clicked away from her research screen to her homework page. The last thing she wanted was to get into a whole theological discussion with her parents. They were brainiacs who were always reading non-fiction junk. They lived for deep, meaningful discussions.

"Come in!"

Her parents opened the door and stepped into her room.

"Hey," Jazz said, trying to find the right balance of sad and happy. Too sad, and a whole 'how are you feeling' talk would ensue. Too happy, and she might be deemed crazy, or heartless, or unstable and in need of professional care.

"Hey, sweetie," her mother said. "We wanted to see how you were holding up after your first day back."

"How are you feeling, baby?" added her father. "You okay?"

Sigh.

"I'm okay," Jazz lied, and then, taking note of the sight frowns on her parents' faces, she quickly added, "I mean, it's hard. Weird. You know? I keep wanting to call Landi and tell her things or ask her opinion. It sucks. A lot." The lump immediately reappeared in her throat. She snatched a tissue and wiped away the tears, all the while avoiding looking directly at her parents.

"We know it's going to be hard, baby," her mother said. "You can always come talk to us. You don't have to deal with this alone."

"I miss her like I'm missing an arm," Jazz sobbed. This was why she didn't want to talk about it. Talking about it turned on the faucet of grief which threatened to drown her. The steady drip of sorrow she could deal with but talking led to the torrent of pain. She was pretty sure that if she thought too much about how much she missed Landi, she would go insane. Stark, raving mad.

Through blurry eyes, she saw the deep sadness and concern etched on her parents' faces. Her throat burned from the lump in it. She swallowed convulsively, trying desperately to maintain control over herself.

After a moment, she forced herself to look up at her parents and gave them a shrug. Her mother sat biting her lip, looking like she was trying to keep calm. Her father was clenching his teeth together, his jaw muscles flexing. Something he did when he was upset.

Oh great. Too much honesty. Now I'm in for it, a long talk about what happened. What it means. Why God does what he does. I can't take it.

Much to her relief, her parents simply came over and hugged her hard, saying nothing.

"We know how awful this is going to be for you," her mother said quietly. "And we want to let you know that we love you and will be here whenever you need us, for whatever you need us for."

Jazz nodded, her throat too clogged with emotion for her to utter any words. So, focused on herself, she'd never even thought about how this all affected her parents. They had loved Landi too. Jazz pulled away from them and grabbed a tissue to wipe her face. She handed one to her mother, who needed one too. Her father, his mouth pinched together tightly, was looking down at his shoes. Jazz's stomach clenched. Seeing her father trying to reign in his heartache was almost too much for her to handle. She turned away from them both, busying herself with folding the pile of giveaway clothes from her closet.

"Okay, well, you should head to bed," her mother said once she'd regained her composure. "And Jazz, please consider talking to Dr. Watkins. Therapy's nothing to be ashamed of. Good night, get some rest. It's getting late."

Jazz spun back around, looked at the clock on her laptop, and frowned. "Late? It's only, like, 9:15?"

Not to mention the fact that her parents hadn't told her when to go to bed since middle school.

"Yes, but I read an article on grief that said getting sleep helps the healing process. We don't want you up at night getting tired and getting sadder and sadder. Depression and poor sleeping patterns go hand in hand. Maybe you should shut it down for tonight. It's only a suggestion, of course."

Jazz suppressed a groan. Her mother's stupid sociology journals were the bane of her existence since birth.

"Um..." Jazz quickly weighed her options in her head before answering. She could, one, argue with them, which would be her pre-accident Jazz way. Or, two, let her parents win this one tiny battle and hope that this will be the extent of their meddling.

"Fine. I'll head to bed now. If that's what the all-knowing Journal of Modern Sociology suggests." She infused as much sarcasm and snark into the sentence as she could.

The surprised but satisfied look on her parents' faces let her know that she'd made the right decision and answered in a way that relieved a lot of their worry.

Unfortunately, in keeping with her parents' research, all Jazz did rather than fall blissfully asleep was lay in bed, tossing and turning as she tried to come up with a plan of action to earn absolution. And even though nothing came to mind, her mind started racing.

Why couldn't she figure out a plan? She could always come up with a plan. At least she could plan fun. She wasn't used to trying to figure out how to serve others.

What she needed was Landi. This was definitely a Landi situation. If she hadn't died (you mean if you hadn't killed her reminded the nasty voice), Landi would be stock full of ideas for how to go about helping others and winning her way back to heaven. Jazz was only useful when planning a bowling party or some other frivolous but totally fun and awesome bit of nonsense.

Missing Landi got her thinking about when she'd ever see her again. She'd never thought about death or the afterlife or heaven before. And she'd spent the last few years trying to get out of going to church as much as possible. Still, even the one or two times a month she did go, she didn't remember the sermons talking about anything like this before. Then again, she did listen all that much to the sermons. She was pretty sure that Landi would have gone straight to heaven. Isn't that what they said about kids? That they went straight to heaven? Was Landi considered a kid? She'd already turned 17.

A sob escaped Jazz. 17. Landi was only 17. Landi would never be 18. Unable to stand it anymore, Jazz sat up and turned on her light. Grabbing the last of the tissues from the box, she wiped her tears and blew her nose. Noting that her nose now felt like it did days into a head cold, raw from being blown.

She searched briefly for her phone, wanting to put on some music. Something to distract her. It took a moment for her to remember that she didn't have her phone. Hadn't seen it since it was on the floor behind Landi. Both of their hands reaching for it.

She thought briefly of getting up and turning on her laptop, but maybe music wasn't something she should be allowed to enjoy. Maybe God wanted her to think about what she'd done and how she was going to make it to heaven to see Landi again.

Finally, after an hour of flipping and flopping around in her bed, Jazz fell asleep — still without a plan in place, and still, as far as she was concerned, on her way straight to hell.

CHAPTER ELEVEN
LIVING FOR THE WEEKEND

Friday wasn't much easier than Thursday had been. Acting like her old self was proving to be a bigger challenge than ever. She simply could not remember how to be energetic and chipper, and talkative anymore. Not to mention witty and friendly and funny. It was exhausting being the old Jazz Sanders, and frankly, her heart was not in it. Not only that, but the new Jazz felt like she was on an emotional rollercoaster. First, she'd be irritated when people wanted to talk about Landi and the accident. Then the next minute, she'd feel annoyed and disgusted by the people who didn't bring Landi up at all and talked about unimportant crap. Trying to mask these oscillating feelings with the expected jovial Jazz demeanor left her feeling drained and cranky. By the end of the school day, all she could do was stand with her head inside her locker (yes, inside, because the smell reminded her of Landi, and she didn't care how crazy she looked). As streams of students passed behind her chatting happily about their Friday night plans, Jazz stood alone by (well, halfway inside) her locker and tried to figure out what she was going to do that weekend — the first of an eternity of weekends without Landi. What was she going to do with herself, by herself, all weekend long?

"What are you doing this weekend?"

Whoa, did I say that out loud?

"Hello! Earth to Jazz!"

Jazz reluctantly withdrew her head from the locker and turned to see Brandon standing there grinning his stupid sexy grin at her.

"What is this, like some type of test or something? Like Jesus in the wilderness?" Jazz asked the Lord, her head tilted up toward the ceiling. "Or was he tempted in the desert? Mountaintop? I forget."

"Huh?" Brandon looked up at the ceiling too. "I'm lost. A test? You're going camping or something this weekend?"

"No, never mind, I wasn't talking to you? Please repeat the question, kind sir."

"You, this weekend, plans?"

"Oh, me, this weekend, plans. Um, let's see. Nothing? Yeah, that's right. I've a whole lot of nothing going on this weekend. I, oh crap, I'm scheduled to cheer at the soccer game on Saturday afternoon. But that's it."

"You cheerleaders go to soccer games?"

"Oh, you think only you big shots on the basketball team are the only school athletes worthy of our awesome cheerleading skills?"

"Nah, nah, it ain't like that. I was, you know, surprised, is all. I mean, it's soccer, and girls' soccer, too. I thought you guys just cheered for dudes."

"Wow. Sexist much? Well, to be honest, only half the squad goes at a time, so we rotate. And need I remind you that, unlike some teams, our girls' soccer won state last year. So, some might say they are more worthy of our talents than say a team that lost in the first round of playoffs."

"Wow. That's cold. At least we got to state this year. Anyway, I was wondering if you wanted to catch a movie tonight or something."

"Catch a movie, which one is running? Ha! Get it, catch a movie, running. Get it?"

Brandon grinned at her, which made her toes seriously tingle. Her toes and every single body part from her pinky toe up. Jazz ignored the pleasant feelings. Feeling all goosebumpy and tingly was too much of a betrayal to her mourning and made her feel even guiltier and way too much alive. She was an awful person to feel like that.

"All jokes aside, how 'bout it? I'll even pay for popcorn."

Jazz opened her mouth to answer before snapping it shut again because a thought shot like a lightning bolt, unbidden, across her mind, leaving her speechless and faintly nauseous. For the thousandth time that day, her eyes filled with tears. She didn't bother to fake a sneeze and complain about allergies this time. She was too tired to try and pretend to be anything but sad.

A frown of confusion crossed Brandon's face.

"You okay? Don't like popcorn or what? Nachos? M&M's?"

Jazz swallowed the lump that was making her throat ache.

"Nothing, I," she muttered, trying to muster up a quick, witty retort to his popcorn comment. Instead, much to her dismay, a sob escaped. Her hand flew to her mouth to try and stifle the sound, but it was too late. Brandon heard it, and so did a group of seniors who had stopped close to them.

Brandon's face morphed from confusion to concern, which of course, made her feel even worse. The seniors turned and looked at her curiously. Brandon pulled her gently out of their hearing distance.

"You know, Jazz," he said softly. "You don't have to keep up that brave, cheerful front with me. I told you that yesterday. You can be real with me."

Jazz, who was studying her shoes, nodded. Unless she was going to go running back to Father Peter, she needed to be able to tell someone at least a few things. Besides, as far as she knew, Brandon wasn't a noisy gossip. Lately, there were times when she felt so much emotion and was filled with so many unsaid things inside her, she thought she'd explode.

She took a deep breath to steady her voice and said quietly, "It's that I was about to say that Ty and Landi should double with us, is all. For that brief second, I forgot. And then when I remembered... it's like a punch in the stomach."

Brandon's eyebrows shot up.

"Damn, that's deep."

Jazz nodded and then shrugged before admitting, "I haven't gotten the hang of thinking for one. I've been thinking for two for so long. It's a habit."

Brandon nodded. "Yeah, you and Landi were definitely joined at the hip."

Jazz simply smiled in agreement before turning away from him and pulling her books and purse out of her locker. An unbidden thought floated across her mind.

If only he had asked her to the movies last week, then Landi would still be alive, the annoying little voice in her head said sadly. If he had wanted to go to the movies last Friday instead of that stupid party, then things would have been different today. A grimace flitted across Jazz's face at the thought. A stab of pure sadness turned the grimace to a frown. Last week, a movie date would mean that she'd be coming up with a time schedule and places to go before the movie, and Landi? Landi would be fussing, as usual, saying they couldn't do anything until at least 7:00. Landi was always making Jazz wait around until 7 on Fridays because Landi was always at ... Oh my God! That's it!

"Holy shit! That's it!" Jazz shouted out loud, causing the group of seniors to look over at her again and making Brandon jump a little at her sudden outburst.

"Um, I'm so confused now. Again. What's it? I mean, are you saying yes, and that's it, or no, or what? I'm lost," Brandon asked, turning his broad back against the eyes of the other students, using his muscles and brawn to shield Jazz from their curious stares.

But Jazz was too excited by her sudden epiphany to care about what others were thinking. She grinned up at Brandon. "I can't do anything tonight with you."

"Okay, that's cool. I mean, but you don't have to sound so happy about it, though," Brandon muttered. "Can I hit you up tomorrow and see what you got going? I mean, if that's okay."

Jazz gave him a hearty pat on his arm, resisting the urge to squeeze it and tease him about the bulging rock-solid bicep she could clearly feel through his jacket.

"Yep, sure, give me a call tomorrow. I'll be free tomorrow. But tonight, I'm volunteering at Children's Hospital."

Against her better judgment, Jazz allowed Brandon to walk her to the parking lot, not bothering to pay attention to what charming but utterly unimportant things he was saying. Her mind was suddenly so full of new ideas that her body barely reacted when he gave her a warm hug goodbye with a promise to text her Saturday afternoon. Jazz hopped into her car and made herself concentrate on driving with her newly found caution. She was completely awash with excitement about her new plan of action and feeling the old familiar bubbly feeling of hyper-ness she always got when she was on the move. She felt herself grin and then immediately shook her head in disgust with herself. She reminded herself of the all the mistakes she made for the past few days. Most importantly, she'd tortured herself and suffered through hours of unnecessary brain damage and emotional distress for no reason. How could she have put herself through such mental pain when the perfect answer, the perfect solution, was right there, courtesy of course, of one Landi Renee Lewis?

She should have known. Even when dead and gone, her best friend still had her back.

CHAPTER TWELVE
LAST FRIDAY, AND EVERY FREAKING FRIDAY FOR THE PAST YEAR

Pulling out of the school parking lot was like driving into the past. As Jazz drove a familiar route, she remembered how all this started.

At the beginning of their sophomore year, both girls were coerced by their parents into participating in the church's Coming of Age program. Jazz endured the yearlong program with a lot of complaining, whining, and moaning. Landi, being Landi, had thrown herself into it with a lot of gusto. Which meant that when they were required to do 10 hours of community service, Jazz volunteered to plant bulbs in the park over a long weekend (working precisely 5 hours each day), while Landi did not only the 10 required hours of volunteer work at the Children's Hospital but continued to volunteer there once a week every week ever since. Not only that, but she volunteered to work there every Friday afternoon for at least three to four hours. Every single Friday.

Friday!

It had driven Jazz up the wall.

Really, what sort of craziness was that? Monday, okay, sure. Heck, Tuesday, Wednesday, and Thursday were fine too. But Friday? That's insanity. Why not go ahead and volunteer Saturday as well if you are going to be all crazy about it? Ever since the nonsense started, Jazz pleaded with Landi to change her volunteer schedule every week to no avail. Landi would not budge. It was maddening. Plus, adding insult to injury, Landi continually asked, begged, cajoled, and/or demanded that Jazz volunteer with her. She'd even gone as far as filling out the application, gathering the references and all the other steps necessary for the program, and announced a few weeks ago that Jazz was properly vetted to work with the kids at the hospital. Somewhere in a stack of other unimportant papers piled on Jazz's desk in her bedroom was a letter of acceptance from the hospital's youth volunteer program coordinator.

However, despite all Landi's leg work, constant wheedling, and incessant whining, Jazz steadfastly refused to go with her to work at the hospital. In fact, they had a standing argument/discussion about it every Friday afternoon, usually right after school in front of their locker. It was almost a tradition. The argument would begin approximately one second after Landi would ask Jazz for a lift to the hospital. Sometimes these discussions could get heated, especially on those Fridays when Landi's magnanimity got in the way of Jazz's fun and exciting plans for the two of them.

Jazz slowed to a complete stop at a stop sign and shook her head as she remembered their last "discussion" about how Landi's volunteering was always putting a major cramp on Jazz's plans for their social life. A week ago, last Friday afternoon, as they walked from their sweet-smelling locker to Jazz's car.

"Look, girlie, it's only one single Friday night. Just this once. Can't you bail on the sickies for one measly Friday afternoon?" Jazz had whined. "I mean, didn't you tell me that most of the kids who go there change week to week, anyway. It's not like they'd be missing you or anything. Just this once. Please, please, please! Ty's going to be there! And he asked me specifically if you were coming! You know you've been trying to hook up with him for a while."

Landi grinned at her while shaking her head stubbornly. "Nope, no can do. Not even for fine-ass Ty. And I've told you countless times I'm not in the room for the sick kids. I'm in the room for their brothers and sisters. Of course, if you would ever come with me to help, you'd know that. Or at least remember it since I've told you umpteen billion times."

"Yeah, yeah, whatever. You're killin' me, chica, you are killin' me. Come on! You and Ty, me and Brandon, it's the bomb situation! Even if it is at the Wash. Outside, in nature, with trees and animals and other crap. One time only, call in sick. I'm begging you."

Laughing, Landi continued to shake her head. "I am not killing you, and you are forgetting commitments of your own. First of all, you have to cheer this afternoon, so you won't be ready to go anywhere until at least 8:00 or so, anyway, unless you plan to stand around tonight, freezing your ass off in your cheerleading uniform. It's March. Just because it was 75 today doesn't mean it won't be snowing tonight. 'Cause Colorado. And second, you can always go without me, and I'll have one of my brothers pick me up, and I'll meet you there. And thirdly, you know Brandon and Ty won't be there on time, anyway."

Jazz shook her head in frustration even though Landi was right about everything she'd said.

"A, I'm not strollin' up in a party without you. That'd be lame. And B, um, whatever, there is no B. Fine. I'll drop your stank booty off at the stupid Children's Hospital, as usual, again. Like I do every freakin' Friday since forever, and I'll wait patiently until you're done getting your stinkin' Florence Henderson on. Oh, there is a B. It's the 28th, so it might as well be April. And April means spring!"

"Nightingale."

"Huh?"

"The nurse you are trying to refer to is Florence Nightingale, you said Henderson, who is the Brady Bunch mom. And two, spring starts in March, and you know full well Miss I was born here, that it can snow damn near into June. And three, and please say it with me. 'I'm not hanging with the sick kids.'"

"Whatev'," Jazz had said as she'd pulled up in the hospital driveway. She watched Landi gather her things. "Leave your backpack. I'll come grab you after the meet, and we can head to your house and change for the party there. I'm going to grab my cheerleading bag before heading to the stadium. Ugh, I hate cheering for track. We don't even cheer. Just sit there and yell, 'Go! Run! Great job.' It's silliness."

"Poor cheerleader, having to cheer," teased Landi, rubbing her thumb and forefinger together. "My violin's playing a very mournful tune for you and your hard, sad life."

"You are so hateful. No later than 8:30 this time! Last week I waited like 20 minutes out here for you."

"We'll see! Bye Jazzypoo!"

"Lates Landiloo!"

• •

Jolted back to the present by the honk from the car behind her, Jazz turned the corner and parked. In front of Landi's house.

She sat gripping the steering wheel until her hands ached, staring at Landi's house. She didn't know how many minutes passed, but at long last, she gathered up her courage and walked to the front door. Reaching the front porch left her in a quandary.

Before Landi would have known she was on her way and left the door propped open or unlocked. A week ago, she would have simply opened the door, stuck her head in, and announced, "Hello Lewis's, your favorite teen is here! Let the celebration begin!" Or something as equally obnoxious and sassy.

Then, depending on which Lewis was within earshot, she would have received any number of amusing retorts and comebacks. But that was a week ago. A lifetime ago. Today, Jazz stood on the front porch trying to summon the courage to ring the doorbell. She took a deep breath and raised her hand when the door swung open, and she was face-to-face with Mrs. Lewis.

"Girl, I know you weren't about to ring my bell."

Jazz's stomach clenched. Her eyes searched the woman's face for a clue. Mrs. Lewis was looking back at her, unsmiling. She knew! Mrs. Lewis had finally figured out that it was Jazz's driving that killed her daughter.

"Um," Jazz began but stopped, still trying to decipher the look on Mrs. Lewis' face before answering. "Did you say, 'I know YOU weren't about to ring my bell' or 'I KNOW you weren't about to ring my bell?' or 'I know you weren't about to ring MY bell?' Cause I have different witty, yet insightful and clever, replies for each inflection."

Jazz waited a beat. Being clever was her default. She hoped it was the right tone.

Mrs. Lewis smiled, flung the screen door open, and pulled Jazz into a tight hug. Jazz went limp with relief before returning the hug. They stood holding each other for much longer than ever before. Finally, Mrs. Lewis released her and pulled her inside with one hand while wiping a tear away with the other.

"Girl, you are so silly!" Mrs. Lewis said, giving Jazz a final squeeze. "It's sooo good to see you! I was afraid you would disappear from our lives. And then it would have been like we lost two daughters instead of one. I was gonna give you a whole week before I went and hunted you down. I've missed you, you know. I was hoping I'd still get to see that beautiful face of yours around here."

"Well, I wasn't sure...." Jazz began, but Mrs. Lewis continued to talk over her, leading her into the kitchen and handing her an apple. "I know you're hungry. You're always hungry. Here. I was saying to Gene the other day that I'm surprised by the strange things I miss. Like her singing in the mornings to that awful radio station you guys listen to, and her and Roland arguing over the breakfast cereal in the morning, her daily whining about not having a car to drive, and you walking all up in my house like you lived here. And those notes she'd write in the steam on the mirror in the mornings nagging me about whatever it was I was supposed to do for her that day. God, I really miss those. Every time I step out of the shower, I automatically look over to see what she wrote."

Suddenly, Mrs. Lewis let out a sob and pulled Jazz into another tight hug. "Thank you so much for coming by, although I know you were not about to ring my bell. I could not believe it when I saw you standing on the porch like you was some stranger! Wildin' out. Isn't that what you guys say? You were wilding out."

Jazz stammered, "It's that... I didn't know whether I... I guess I was thinking of something else to say instead of my usual clever greeting. I thought maybe it would be best to ring the doorbell. I don't know..." Jazz's voice trailed off. She swallowed down a sob of her own before looking at Mrs. Lewis with a lame little smile.

Mrs. Lewis gave her one last squeeze before letting her go.

"Girl, please. You ain't rang our doorbell since you was about 10 years old. No use in starting up again now. Okay, kiddo, spill it."

Jazz's stomach flipped. "Spill what?"

"Tell me why you're here. As much as I'd like to, I will not disillusion myself into believing that you are here to hang out with me. As much as I'd like that."

Jazz smiled. "Whatev' Mrs. L. You know you're too busy to want to kick it with a 16-year-old. In fact," Jazz said, looking Mrs. Lewis up and down. "Based on your cute outfit, I'd bet that you and Mr. L are headed to, wait, let me guess, the usher fun night at the church. Isn't it tonight?"

"Smart aleck. Yes, but we are going to dinner first because Mrs. Warren is making the dinner for the ushers, and you know she can't boil water. And this is the first time we've been out since, well, since Landi. It just doesn't feel right going out to something called a "fun night." I feel like I should be sitting at home doing... I don't know what, but something besides trying to have some fun. People keep saying it will make me feel better, to get out, get my mind off it. I can't imagine how they think playing Bid Whist will make me forget I've lost my baby girl. Nothing will make me feel better. Ever." Mrs. Lewis turned away.

Jazz looked down at her shoes as the familiar ache of sadness and guilt reappeared in her throat. For a moment, she and Mrs. Lewis stood quietly, lost in their own thoughts. With a swift wipe of her cheeks, Mrs. Lewis took a deep breath as if forcibly pushing away the sadness and gave Jazz a smile. Jazz could see the effort it took for Mrs. Lewis to do so and wondered if that's how she looked all day while at school, like she was visibly putting on a brave face as if donning a mask. She hoped not; it was painful to watch; it was clear that the mask didn't reach Mrs. Lewis' eyes.

"Anyway, what's up, darling girl? Did you leave something here?" Mrs. Lewis continued. Her voice was falsely chipper, her smile cheerfully fake. She reached over and took Jazz's hand. "You doing okay? I know this is hard for you, too. You two were as close as sisters."

Oh-oh, the conversation was veering into dangerous territory, aka Jazz's feelings and thoughts. And it was very dangerous territory indeed since Jazz had only been there a few minutes, and already she was feeling the urge to confess her sins and beg this woman for forgiveness. The last thing she wanted was for Mrs. and Mr. Lewis to ever find out that she was the blame for Landi's death. Jazz didn't think she could take it if they hated her for the rest of her life. Even if that was exactly what she deserved. Their absolute, unforgiving hatred.

"Well, I'm actually here to pick up Landi's SibSanc bag," she said, looking around for the bag that Landi always carried to school and then to the hospital on Fridays, glad for the legitimate reason to change the subject.

"Really?" Mrs. Lewis said, looking so shocked that Jazz felt slightly insulted. "Is that so? The SibSanc sack?"

"Yeah, I figured, since Landi won't be, can't, you know," she stammered. "I thought I'd go and see if they need volunteers."

"Hmmm," Mrs. Lewis said, looking at Jazz with a slight frown. "You don't say? Hpmh."

"What? Is that a bad idea?" Jazz's heart sank. She'd thought it was the perfect answer to her problem, but she wouldn't go if Mrs. Lewis thought she shouldn't.

"No, no, it's a fine idea. A great idea, for a lot of different reasons. It's only that I can recall, oh I don't know, maybe a thousand conversations, no wait conversation is not the right word, a thousand loud, whiny arguments, I've overheard a billion times between you and Landi. She'd be demanding that you volunteer with her at the hospital and you would be adamantly refusing to do so. Which, I have to say, is one of the things I always liked about you, your ability to stand up to Landi. She can be so… oh. I mean, she could be so bossy. She is the youngest, but she can boss around every single one of her older brothers. Was the youngest. It is, I mean, was ridiculous the way they kowtowed to that girl… Landi is… She was something else…."

Jazz frowned. She didn't like anyone talking badly about Landi, even if it was her own mother. Ignoring the flash of irritation she felt at Landi's mother pointing out Landi's faults, she gave Mrs. Lewis' a smile she didn't mean. She tried to force the smile up into her eyes but knew she'd failed. Like Mrs. Lewis' smile, she knew hers hadn't traveled further than her mouth either. After a moment of giving each other bogus smiles, they both dropped them as if the effort of pulling the corners of their mouths up was too hard to sustain.

"I know. I was so not into it. But now, I don't know." Jazz shrugged, trying to find the words to explain herself without talking about absolution, mercy, charity, or going to hell. "I kinda thought it would be a good idea. A tribute, maybe, I don't know. But if you think I shouldn't go...."

"As I said, it's a great idea. I think you'll be wonderful at it actually," she laughed a little. "Probably better than Landi even."

Jazz again frowned at Mrs. Lewis as she turned her back, waving Jazz into the foyer and grabbing a blue bag with the word 'SibSanc' bedazzled on the front of it.

"Here you go, kiddo! The world-famous SibSancSack. Enjoy!"

"Thank you," Jazz said softly, wondering at the weight of the sparkly bag. Her eyes filled as she realized she had no idea what was inside the bag. All this time and she'd never thought to ask. She blinked quickly, trying to clear her tears before looking up at her best friend's mother. Mrs. Lewis's face, usually so animated and bright, looked still and ashen. Jazz took a shuddering breath. Immediately, Mrs. Lewis stepped forward and pulled Jazz into yet another tight, long hug.

"Don't be a stranger, Jazzypoo. I mean it. I love seeing your face," she whispered. She held Jazz at arm's length and looked at her intently before saying, "And don't try to be a saint, either. You're a good kid. Always have been. You keep doing you. Don't try and be anyone else."

"Yes, ma'am," Jazz answered, confused by Mrs. Lewis's last comment. "I will. Have fun tonight. See ya, Sunday."

Mrs. Lewis burst out laughing, almost sincerely this time. "Yeah, right! I haven't seen you in church in forever. I must have sucker written across my forehead."

Jazz trotted down the porch stairs to her car, trying to figure out how she felt about Mrs. Lewis's parting comment. She was halfway to the hospital before she decided that yes, in fact, she was insulted by it.

• •

For the first time, Jazz had to park her car at the hospital instead of simply dropping Landi off. When she pulled up to the parking garage, a flash flood of exasperation washed over her because she would have to pay for parking, and her immediate instinct was to back up and go home. She'd actually put her car into reverse before remembering that this was about absolution, not the $2 flat parking fee.

The Children's Hospital was unlike any hospital Jazz had ever been in. The atrium felt airy and light, and the colors were bright and sunny. One continuous mural filled with famous literary and fantasy characters covered the walls that led up to the information desk. Despite the year of Landi's volunteering there, Jazz never set foot inside the building with her, and she'd no idea where to go.

"Excuse me, Miss, but I'm looking for the SibSanc. Can you tell me how to get there?"

"I'm sorry, the what?" The person sitting at the information desk looked as confused as Jazz felt.

"The, um, SibSanc?"

"I'm sorry, I'm not sure what you're talking about."

Jazz stared down at the clerk. The clerk stared back. Then it dawned on Jazz. Landi had a nickname for everybody and everything. Obviously, "SibSanc" was another pet name, courtesy of Landi's creative brain. Jazz smiled to herself despite the pang of sadness and longing that she felt.

"Sorry, the real name is the, um, shoot, I forgot." Jazz wracked her brain, trying to remember the proper name for the area. "Let's see, I think it's called the Sibling... spot?"

"Oh! SibSanc. That's cute," the clerk grinned. "You are looking for The Brooks Memorial Sibling Sanctuary. Yes, of course. Are you here visiting a patient, or are you one of our volunteers?"

"Oh, I'm a volunteer. I didn't bring my letter of acceptance, though. Should I run home and get it?" Deep down, Jazz hoped that the clerk would give her an out. She'd run home and not come back. But the clerk didn't. Instead, she smiled happily up at Jazz and said, "No, no. All I need is your driver's license. I need to verify you are in our system."

Jazz handed her ID over and watched the clerk type her information into the computer. As she waited, Jazz's thoughts swung from hoping that she'd be turned away so she could go home to being scared she'd be refused entry and then would have to start all over trying to figure out a new way to heaven. But after a moment, the clerk said, "There you are! Ms. Jazz Lynn Sanders. Jazz, wow, cool name. Okay, Jazz, let me print out a volunteer tag for you. Look into my camera there. Give me a smile. Great. Okay, here you go. You are now official."

Jazz looked down at her brand-new badge. It was still warm from the printer. The photo looked sad. Her smile hadn't reached her eyes.

"Okay, great, thank you. So which way?"

"Follow the duck feet."

"I'm sorry. Follow the what?"

The information clerk smiled and stood up at the desk, leaned over, and pointed down to the floor. Starting from in front of the desk, yellow duck feet were painted on the floor that headed down one hallway. A set of brown bear prints led in the opposite direction, and blue hoof prints circled around the desk and continued straight ahead.

"Follow the duck feet to the very end of the hall. You can't miss the sign, Peter Pan's right above the doorway."

"Okey-dokey, then," Jazz said. "Thank you."

"No, thank you. We don't get enough teen volunteers around here!"

Jazz gave her a vague smile and a half-hearted wave before turning and following the sunny yellow duck feet, all the while hoping that they would lead her straight to her soul's redemption.

CHAPTER THIRTEEN
A PROMISE OF SANCTUARY

Jazz followed the cheery yellow duck prints to the Peter Pan painting, took a deep breath, and opened the door. She wasn't sure what she was expecting. Despite the many stories and descriptions Landi gave her, she'd never created a mental picture of the space. What she saw surprised her. Rather than the generic playroom, she was expecting, Jazz felt as though she'd walked into a mini fantasy world. Whoever the Brooks Family was, they either had deep pockets or big hearts, probably based on the spread before her, both.

To her right was an area that was clearly created for little girls with princess fantasies. A faux castle gate led into an area that was a riot of pinks and purples. A play kitchen was to the right, complete with a couple of cute little tables and chairs, a big bin of stuffed animals, and a box overflowing with dolls of all sizes. To the side of the box was a huge dollhouse that probably reached to Jazz's shoulder if she were close to it. A miniature French doorway led to a space whose floor was completely covered with bean bags and cushions, in varying shades of pink and purple, surrounding a flat-screen television mounted to the wall. Currently, two little girls were watching the movie *Frozen*. Scratch that. One girl was watching the movie, eyes riveted to the screen, mouth hanging slightly open, while the other was crashed, curled up like a little mouse in the middle of a sea of pink cushions.

Looking to the left of the doorway, Jazz saw the designated boy area, complete with a fake pirate ship. Climbing nets led up to the crow's nest, with a couple of slides providing an alternative way down. Their television area was tucked in the back through a couple of miniature dungeon doors that opened into a bunch of black and gray bean bags, as well as a gangplank, with a cushion covered in a material made of skull and crossbones. Off to the side was an extensive racetrack. No one was around to watch the *Transformers* video that was playing.

Directly opposite the door, through a doorway painted to resemble jungle vines, was a space that Jazz assumed was for the older kids. A couple of old-school pinball machines stood next to a couple of newer video games. In the back corner stood a television with a Nintendo console hooked up to it. In the other corner were three round tables with chairs, surrounded by shelves with various arts and crafts, puzzles, and board games. Double glass doors opened into a bricked-in courtyard with a couple of tables and a large grassy area with ample room to toss a ball around, which was what the only other two kids she saw were doing.

"Hello there, may I help you?"

Jazz turned around to see a smiling, elderly woman bustling over to her. An unbidden smile broke over Jazz's face. There was something about the short, round, brown-skinned woman that made you want to smile back at her. Jazz knew all about her from Landi. A bundle of sunshine she'd called the older woman. And Landi hadn't given this woman a nickname, saying that her real name spoke volumes already. A clear sign Landi liked her quite a bit.

"Hello, you must be Grandma Daisy," Jazz said, smiling and extending her hand. "I'm Jazz Sanders. I've come to volunteer."

"Oh, my word!" Grandma Daisy's smile got bigger, and she threw up her hands in excitement. "I don't believe it. I have heard your name. I don't know how many times from Landi. Come here and give Grandma Daisy a hug!"

Jazz reached down and hugged the woman, who smelled faintly like vanilla and baking bread.

"Wow, you smell great!" Jazz said, pulling herself out of the hug. "But now I'm hungry."

Grandma Daisy beamed up at her and laughed. "Child, I've spent all day in my kitchen baking for a program at my church. I can't tell you how many cookies and rolls I made today. I must have vanilla in my blood and yeast in my skin! Now, where is Miss Landi? I know she's the one responsible for you being here."

Jazz's smile melted off her face. Grandma Daisy's face morphed into a picture of concern.

"Honey, what is it? She okay?"

Jazz shook her head. She swallowed a couple of times.

"Landi, we got, she's…." Jazz said thickly. This was the first time she would have to tell someone who knew how wonderful Landi was that she was dead. Unlike her talk with Father Peter when she couldn't have stopped the words from coming out of her mouth if she wanted to, with Grandma Daisy, no words would come. Finally, after a moment, Jazz looked away from the worry etched on the old woman's face and spoke instead to her shoes. "Landi was in a car accident a week ago. Friday night."

"Sweet Jesus," Grandma Daisy said. She clasped a hand to her heart. "Is she okay? Is she somewhere upstairs? A different hospital?"

Swallowing again, Jazz shook her head. She looked up, past the woman's face, and spoke instead to the crown of gray hair. "Landi's gone, ma'am. She passed away."

"Dear God, that sweet girl. My word."

Grandma Daisy walked over to a desk and sat in a chair. She leaned back and closed her eyes. "I didn't know. I didn't hear. I've been back home in Georgia last weekend and all this week. I just got back yesterday. I didn't know. Oh, Landi. Lord, that beautiful child, gone." Grandma Daisy bowed her head, clasping her hands together.

Jazz could feel the sadness radiating off Grandma Daisy in waves. The feeling dug right into her heart, and she immediately began to cry, as if the old woman had reached inside of her and turned on a spigot.

"Oh child, I'm so sorry, don't cry, baby. Landi's in heaven now. She's in a better place. We're the ones who are feeling pain and sorrow. Landi's free of this world's troubles."

Grandma Daisy reached towards a box of tissues and handed Jazz a wad. That this woman was trying to comfort her made Jazz feel worse. Grandma Daisy pulled off her glasses and dabbed her own tear-filled eyes.

"My Landi is up there singing and dancing with Jesus... Lord, have mercy. I've gotten so used to comforting my little ones in their grief and sadness, I've forgotten what it feels like to have those feelings myself. Sweet Jesus, give me strength. My word, am I going to miss that child. She was like one of my own grandkids. I just loved her. She was like a little mother to these kids. God bless her."

Grandma Daisy dabbed her eyes again and began to fan herself, rocking back and forth in grief, shaking her head in dismay. Jazz grabbed another tissue and dried her tears as well. At that moment, the little girl from the castle appeared.

"Grandma Daisy?" she said. "I'm hungry. Grandma Daisy? You okay?"

Jazz watched as Grandma Daisy gathered herself together. She could see the older woman center and calm herself. It was as if Jazz could see her physically push away the grief and sadness she clearly felt. Only a few seconds passed before a sincere smile appeared on Grandma Daisy's face, and she took the little girl by the hand. The little girl, who had looked frightened, visibly relaxed and leaned against the older lady, cozying up to her side. Grandma Daisy gathered the little girl in her arms, clearly gaining as much comfort from the little girl as she was giving to the child. Jazz suddenly felt the urge to get another hug from the woman. She wanted some comfort as well. Instead, she angled her face so the little girl couldn't see the tears that were rolling down her cheeks and tried to calm and center herself like Grandma Daisy. It took a great deal of mental strength to do so, and Jazz clearly wasn't as strong as Grandma Daisy. It took a few more minutes before she could stop crying and join the two in the snack bar area.

"Well, Miss Brianna," Grandma Daisy said. "Why don't you do me a big favor and give Miss Jazz here a tour while I rustle up something for you to munch on! Deal?"

The little girl looked up at Jazz uncertainly.

Jazz plastered a smile on her face, "I would really love a tour from an expert! This is my first time here, and I need someone smart to teach me the ropes."

It was the right thing to say because Brianna's face lit up immediately. "Okay, I'll show you. I know where everything is."

Jazz glanced over at Grandma Daisy, who smiled again and nodded approvingly over Brianna's head at Jazz. With a fleeting sad look, Grandma Daisy turned and hustled through a door behind the desk.

"Okay, so over there is the boys' stuff. It's just pirates and ropes and slides and junk. Now over here is our most beautiful fairy castle," said Brianna, grabbing Jazz's hand and pulling her over with more strength than one would expect. Jazz ducked to get through the doorway just in time.

"Here is where you can have tea parties, and here are all the things you need for the tea party. And here is where you can get cozy and watch a movie or sleep like she's doing, although she's the one who got to pick out the movie, which I've seen a zillion million times. And then over here is where you. .. come on. What's your name again?"

"It's Jazz."

"Come on, Miss Jazz," said Brianna, gesturing impatiently for Jazz to follow her out of the castle.

"Oh, you can just call me Jazz. No, Miss necessary."

"Uh, huh. Grandma Daisy says we have to call the old people Miss."

"Well, I'm not really old."

Brianna stopped and looked up at Jazz, her brows furrowed. "Do you have two numbers in your age?"

"Well, yes, I'm 16, but …."

"Do you get to drive a real alive car?"

"Well, yes. Of course, it's not alive."

Brianna frowned. "So, it's not a real alive car?"

"Well, it's a real car, but you know cars aren't alive," Jazz said, explaining her little joke, which had clearly fallen flat.

"But it's a for really car. Not like a play car, right? It's a real car that you drive on a real, alive street?"

Jazz gave up. "Yes, it is."

Brianna threw up her hands in exasperation. "Well, duh, then it's a real alive car. Do you have a real purse with money in it?"

"Um, yes. A real alive one."

"Well then, you are old," Brianna replied with an air of absolute certainty. "Come on, Miss Jazz."

Jazz followed meekly behind the little girl, feeling old.

For the next ten minutes, Brianna showed Jazz the entire SibSanc, focusing on those areas which she deemed important (the arts and crafts area, the Wii station area, as well as a return trip to the castle area for a recap of its better features) and simply waving an unimpressed hand at those areas she found uninteresting. Still, despite the biased tour, Jazz got a good understanding of the Sanctuary from her little guide.

"Well, thank you very much, Brianna. How old are you anyway?"

"6 and three quarters."

"So, you are in, like, kindergarten?"

Brianna frowned up at Jazz, patently annoyed.

"I'm in first grade, and I'm the smartest in my class."

"Of course, first grade. What was I thinking? When you get old like I am, you make mistakes, you know. I'm terribly sorry."

The frown on Brianna's face eased, and she nodded sagely. "Yes, I know. My mommy has the same brain problems. She's old too."

Jazz was about to explain that she was nowhere near as old as Brianna's mother when Grandma Daisy appeared with two plates with apple slices, ham and cheese sandwiches, fruit snacks, and a box of juice.

"Here you go, Brianna, please go wake Hayley up. You two may have your snack at the tea table."

"Thank you, Grandma Daisy!"

"Thank you for the tour, Brianna," Jazz said. "You're an expert."

"Yes, I am. You're welcome, Miss Jazz. If you forget something else, come ask me, and I'll help you remember," called Brianna over her shoulder as she carefully carried the two plates toward the tea party area. "My brain works fine."

Jazz laughed. "Thank you, I will." She turned back to Grandma Daisy with a smile. "She's something else."

Grandma Daisy looked fondly over at Brianna. "Yes, that little girl is too much. She's here often. Her older brother has leukemia, poor thing."

They both watched as Brianna woke up Hayley and then walked over to the tea party area and began arranging their snacks. Once Grandma Daisy saw the girls were settled, she beckoned Jazz over to the desk.

"I'm sorry about earlier. Landi's passing was so unexpected, and it shook me. I was away in Georgia visiting my son and his family. Just got back yesterday. I must have missed the news." Grandma Daisy paused here and sighed sadly. "I've lived for more than seventy years, and I still can't get used to young people passing away. Breaks my heart. That's why I work down here instead of up in one of the playrooms on the patient floors. At any rate, I'll have to send her poor parents a card," Jazz watched Grandma Daisy gather her thoughts again, watched as she again pulled her focus away from the sad news. She marveled at the strength of the older Black woman to center herself. It was a skill that Jazz was going to try and master.

"Okay," Grandma Daisy began, sounding official. "Let me give you an explanation of the Brooks Family Memorial Sibling Sanctuary. First, a very brief history: Paul Brooks is a very successful businessman. When Mr. Brooks was a child, his brother Don got a rare form of cancer. For years, Paul would have to accompany his mother to the hospital and spend hours and hours, and days and days, sitting in the waiting room while his mother sat by Don's bedside. Back in those days, most hospitals didn't have play areas, not even for those kids who were in the hospital for treatment. So, for months, while the doctors fought Don's cancer, Paul was forced to sit in the waiting room, or when allowed to, sit quietly in a chair in a corner of Don's room. Well, Paul would later go on and invent a medical device that is not only in every hospital but in most rooms in every hospital. The man's filthy rich. When the children's hospital was being built, he contacted the powers that be and said he wanted to donate a ton of money, but only if he could dictate exactly how it was going to be used. His idea was to create a place where the siblings of sick kids could go and be kids. Remembering what it was like to sit quietly for hours, Paul wanted a playroom that was bright and sunny and where healthy kids could go and be loud and run and jump and sing without being constantly reprimanded by the nurses, doctors, or their own parents to be quiet and still: a space somewhere in the hospital where they would feel welcome. One thing Paul hated most was when the doctors would come in, look over at him sitting in the chair and pull his mother to the side, and whisper. He said it made him feel like an intruder; like he was someone unwanted. A nuisance.

That is why he created a sanctuary for siblings. What you see in front of you, the castle, the pirate ship, the teen spot, the courtyard, is about two-thirds of the total space. Behind me, through those doors, is a full kitchen, stocked with mostly healthy snacks, although I sneak in a few goodies because children deserve a little treat now and then. A washer and dryer. We wash those stuffed animals every night. Can't be too careful. Also, through that door is a smaller play area and television for those siblings who are sick. Not sick, as in cancer sick, but sniffles, colds, flus, that sort of thing. As well as a quiet room for toddlers, cribs, mats and such for when they are here with their parents during their naptime. They also have their own little play area for kids 4 and younger. Whew. Okay, enough of that. They make us say that to first-time volunteers and... Oh, dear."

At that moment, another older woman came hurrying in, looking irritated and flustered. Grandma Daisy paused in her story and looked over at the woman.

"Good afternoon, Ruth," she said pleasantly.

"Sorry, I'm late. The traffic is awful this time of day," huffed the older woman. "Wasn't my fault. I left the house with plenty of time. Who's this?"

Jazz stepped forward and extended her hand. "Good afternoon, I'm Jazz Sanders. I'm volunteering today."

The older woman who stood rigidly before them was the visual opposite of Grandma Daisy. Miss Ruth was pale, thin, and angular, while Grandma Daisy was brown, plump, and round.

She gave Jazz's hand a wary look before grabbing only the tips of her fingers and giving them a perfunctory shake. Then the woman immediately turned and squirted a large glop of antibacterial gel in her hands from the industrial-sized bottle sitting on the desk. After rubbing her hand vigorously together, she turned her back on them both, opened one of the desk drawers, grabbed an antibacterial wipe, and began cleaning the keyboard, computer, and desk, with a tense and surly look on her face.

Surprised, Jazz looked over at Grandma Daisy. Grandma Daisy rolled her eyes and gave her a wink. Jazz smothered a laugh as Landi's nickname for this other woman popped into her head. GG. Short for Germophobic Grinch.

"This is Mrs. Reeves," Grandma Daisy said to Jazz. "She mostly mans the desk."

Jazz nodded, not at all surprised since she couldn't see Mrs. Reeves interacting with the kids. Mrs. Reeves looked up and gave Jazz a curt nod before returning to her disinfecting.

"Ruth, I'm going to show Jazz the back area for a minute. Can you keep an eye on Brianna and Hayley?

They are having their snack in the castle. Oh, and Leonard and Dom are playing football in the courtyard."

Mrs. Reeves looked over at the two girls who were, at the moment, clicking their juice boxes together as if they had just finished a toast. She scowled. "Why are they eating there instead of at the tables or in the courtyard?" she snapped. "They'll make a mess!" She looked accusingly at Jazz. Jazz instinctively took a step closer to Grandma Daisy.

"I told them they could have a tea party," answered Grandma Daisy evenly. "They are the only ones here. Brianna will not allow them to make a mess. It will be fine."

Mrs. Reeves shook her head disapprovingly. "I'll call custodial services and have them come sanitize and vacuum the area."

"Sound idea, Ruth," Grandma Daisy said. "Sound idea. Jazz, come with me."

Jazz followed her through a doorway, closing the door softly behind her.

"Don't mind Ruth," Grandma Daisy said cheerfully. "She's a fussy old biddy. I make her stay behind the desk and check kids in, mostly. She's been bounced from one department in the hospital to another. No one wants to deal with her."

"I can't imagine why," muttered Jazz. "She's lovely."

Grandma Daisy burst out laughing.

"Well, I'll grant you that even though her labor is free, it comes with a price. I don't let it bother me too much, though. Unearned suffering and all that. Besides, I consider it extra credit."

"Huh?"

"Oh, you know, just in case there's a point system for getting into heaven, I try and earn a few extra points here and there. You know, just in case."

Jazz smiled. She loved Grandma Daisy already. "Yeah, I know. Just in case."

CHAPTER FOURTEEN
TIME FLIES

It was already 6:45 when Jazz thought to check her watch. She'd assumed that the time would drag, but within her first hour there the number of kids doubled from four to eight, and the next thing she knew there were at least 18 to 20 kids in the SibSanc. After that, as seven o'clock came and went, she stopped trying to keep track.

First, Grandma Daisy asked her to help a couple of kids with a Nintendo game. She'd gotten it going only to be sucked into a couple of games with a pair of nine-year-old boys. When more kids wanted to play, she dragged over a whiteboard and set up a tournament. The kids loved it, and her brackets stopped any fighting over whose turn it was before it could even start. Then she noticed a little girl trying to reach something from the shelves over by the crafts table. Hurrying over, Jazz grabbed the desired kit and sat down to help the little girl get started doing a paint by number, ensuring she draped a smock over the girls' clothes. Another girl, who had been standing looking lost, wandered over, and Jazz persuaded her to make a bracelet with another kit full of beads and string she'd found. Within a few minutes, all the tables in the craft section were filled with kids coloring, painting, and creating. One of the other teen volunteers had shown up and, after a brief introduction, had shown off her outstanding art skills, causing Jazz to drift away from the area, leaving it to the teen with the better abilities.

As she walked over to the castle to see if her services were needed there, she spotted a little girl looking scared to death, clinging to the front door.

"Hi, there!" Jazz said, crouching, so she was at the little girl's level. "I'm Jazz. What's your name?"

"Marin."

"Hi Marin, have you been here before?"

The little girl shook her head.

"Well, come on in. Let me show you around."

Jazz reached her hand out, and, after a heartbeat, the little girl slipped her hand into hers. Together they wandered around, looking for something that the little girl might want to do. Jazz gave her a tour of the castle, but the little girl didn't want to watch the movie, play with dolls, make anything in the kitchen or join the tea party that was going on. They headed over to the pirate ship, but Marin, although she looked interested in the movie playing, declined to stay and watch it, and she wouldn't try climbing up to the crow's nest.

Marin lingered around the crafts table a while but refused to sit down and join in there either. By the way, Marin's hand tightened on Jazz's as they neared the raucous area around the video game tournament. Jazz knew not to even bother asking her if she wanted to be part of the tournament. Jazz was almost out of ideas and wondering how she was going to get free from Marin when suddenly she remembered Landi's SibSanc bag. Jazz had no idea what was in it and now seemed like a good time to find out.

"Come with me, Marin," said Jazz, as if there were another option considering the child was stuck like glue to her side. "I need to grab my goodie bag."

Pulling the SibSanc Sack from the cupboard behind the desk, Jazz took it and Marin over to the quietest corner of the room. Liberating her hand from Marin's grip, she arranged the oversized pillows on the floor and plopped down on them, making herself comfortable. Marin followed suit.

"Okay, kiddo," she said. "Let's see if there is something in this bag that might excite you."

Jazz flipped the bag over and dumped everything out. She looked with interest at the random objects that came tumbling from the bag. The first thing that caught her eye was a Nerf football. She picked it up and looked over at Marin. The little girl wrinkled her nose with distaste. Jazz shoved the football back in the bag. Marin reached down and picked up a tattered paperback book. Jazz recognized it at once. It was Landi's old copy of *A Little Princess*. Landi had had a rather unhealthy love for that book. Marin looked at it with interest.

"Do you want me to read it to you?" Jazz suddenly remembered her misstep with Brianna and quickly added, "Or, you could curl up here and read it to yourself if you'd like."

Marin continued to study the book, her little finger tracing an outline of the girl on the cover. "Maybe."

Jazz scratched her head, pulled her braids into a bun, shrugged, and went back to sifting through the contents of the bag.

"Ooo, Uno cards! I love Uno!" Jazz said. "Wanna play?"

"I don't know how," said Marin. But she laid the book down and began putting the other toys and things back in the bag.

"It's a piece of cake," Jazz said, helping Marin clean up. "You'll be a pro in no time!"

Marin was a quick study and managed to beat Jazz in their second game. By the fourth game, they picked up two new players, and there were seven players and an audience by game nine. It quickly became clear that Marin was the player to beat. When Marin's parents came to get her, she began whining as they approached the group.

"Oh, can't I stay a little while longer?" she moaned, reluctantly getting up. "I'm the reigning Uno champ! I have to stay and protect my title!"

Her parents, who looked tired and worried, shook their heads. "Sweetie, it's late. Your brother is asleep now, so it's a good time to leave," her mother explained. "Plus, we'll be back here early tomorrow so we can be here for his tests."

"We haven't even gotten dinner yet," said her father, draping an arm over Marin's shoulder. "Besides, aren't you the little girl who didn't want to come here at all?"

"It's fun here. Jazz makes it fun." The little girl turned to Jazz, her face so relaxed now, and asked, "Will you be here tomorrow, Jazz?"

Jazz looked up at Marin in surprise.

"Umm."

Her first inclination was to say no, but all the other kids stopped talking and looked up at her, waiting for her to answer.

"Please, Jazz, please?" moaned Marin.

Jazz glanced from the little girl to Marin's parents. Marin's face was lit up and happy, a total change from what it looked like when she first arrived. But it was Marin's parents' faces, which looked tense as if preparing themselves for more bad news, that swayed her.

"Sure. I can come for a little while in the morning, I guess."

"Yay! Okay, bye then!" Marin gave Jazz a hug and walked off happily with her parents. "See ya tomorrow!"

"It will only be for a little while!" called Jazz, unable to stop herself from setting up an easy out. "I won't be able to stay for long!"

Marin looked back and gave a cheerful little wave.

It was then that Jazz checked her watch and was stunned to see that it was almost 8:30. The time had flown by, and she suddenly understood how Landi always seemed to lose track of time when she was here. A wave of fresh guilt washed over her when she thought about how often she'd given Landi a hard time for making her wait. Not to mention the obnoxious phone messages and texts she'd send when she was sitting in her car impatiently waiting for Landi to come out of the hospital. The thought of the tantrums she'd thrown almost every single Friday night for more than a year galled her.

"Jesus," she muttered. "Crap!" Tears filled her eyes.

"Are you okay?" asked a girl sitting next to her, who was shuffling the cards, preparing to deal.

Jazz straightened up and gave the girl a smile. "Oh, I'm okay. I just thought of something that makes me sad."

The girl nodded knowingly. "I feel sad sometimes, too. Whenever I think about how sick my sister is."

"How old is your sister?" Jazz asked, offering one of the spectators Marin's place in the game, grateful that the girl was talking and pulling the attention of the other kids away from her tears.

"She's nine too," replied the girl. "We're twins." She paused a beat before saying quietly. "She's the sick twin. I'm the other one."

Jazz looked up at the words, "the other one." Why not 'the healthy one' or the 'oldest one by a minute'? She opened her mouth to say something, but nothing came to mind.

Luckily, a boy chimed in, saying, "My brother is 13, but he's been sick so much that he looks younger than me. Everyone thinks I'm the oldest 'cause I'm so much bigger than he is. And even though I'm the youngest, he gets all the attention, 'cause he so sick all the time." The frustration he felt showed clearly on the boy's face. Looking around the group, Jazz saw that many of the other kids were nodding as if they could relate to what he was saying, as well as how he was feeling. Still, nothing, no words of wisdom or comfort, came to mind. Jazz stayed silent.

"I get straight A's and play first chair flute in the Children's Symphony Orchestra, but let my sister get a little cut, and suddenly I'm invisible," a girl sitting across the circle from Jazz said. "It doesn't matter how good I am or what great thing I do. If Clara isn't doing well, then I might as well not exist."

A boy next to her laughed, "Yeah, I've gotten straight A's, I've gotten straight F's. I've been suspended for two weeks, and I've been given awards and stuff at school. But it doesn't much matter if you're good or bad, as long as you're healthy. If you're healthy, then the sick one gets the attention."

The flutist smiled at him, "I got the flu once, and I got all the attention for one whole night until my brother got sick the next morning. Then they practically threw cold medicine at me and focused on Ryan again."

The boy shrugged. "Your kid having flu is nothing if your other kid has an inoperable brain tumor. A running nose and fever can't compete with that, you know."

"Playing state in a football championship becomes unimportant if your sister has sickle cell and she goes into crisis. Well, at least it's unimportant to everyone but you," muttered Leonard, the boy who'd been tossing the football around outside when Jazz first arrived.

"Ever have to wait after school for an extra hour because your parents had to rush your brother to the hospital again, and they forgot to come get you or even to arrange a ride?"

Three or four of the other kids smiled ruefully and nodded.

"It's not so bad, as long as it's not dead of winter," reasoned one boy. "That's when it really sucks."

A girl next to him nodded solemnly, then grinned. "It bites, but it got me a cell phone two years younger than my older sister!"

The group laughed in appreciation.

A boy who had been silent during the conversation but listening to every word, his head swinging back and forth as if he were at a tennis match, said, "My little sister is only here to get her tonsils out."

"Wow. You're lucky," said the flutist. "You'll be here one, maybe two times, max, and then never come back. I practically grew up here."

The boy nodded his head. "Yeah, I guess I am lucky," he admitted softly. "I was all mad that they made to come here instead of taking me to laser tag to meet my friends."

"Phish," said the boy. He pointed to the flutist. "Emma and I see each other here at least three, maybe four times a month. This place is pretty cool, but being here so much sucks sometimes."

Emma smiled at the boy. "Yep, Maxwell and I are regulars. Tonight, I'm missing a bowling party. Last month, Maxwell missed something important. What was it again?"

"The championship game for my basketball team," Maxwell answered with a grimace, then he added grimly, "They won without me. I don't even know if that makes me feel better or worse."

Jazz sat quietly, watched, and listened as the conversation continued around her. The Uno game forgotten. The kids held their cards limply in their hands and talked about what it was like to be the healthy one, the kid in the family that could run and jump and laugh and do. She wanted desperately to chime in. To say something wise and deep and meaningful that would make each of the kids feel better, to ease the guilt they all so clearly felt, but nothing popped into her head. No words, no clever sayings, no nothing. Instead, she just listened and occasionally got up from the group to fetch a needed tissue. That was all she could do.

After a while, as the kids were picked up, things quieted down, and the room slowly emptied. When the last of her Uno group left, Jazz leaned back against the cushions, feeling exhausted, physically and mentally. She pulled her knees up, laid her head on her arms, and closed her eyes.

"Well, I must say I am very impressed."

Jazz opened her eyes and looked up at Grandma Daisy. She raised an eyebrow. It took all of what was left of her energy.

Grandma Daisy laughed. She pulled up a chair and plopped down. "Whew, I'm whipped! Friday nights are always the hardest."

"Really?"

"Well, yes. Parents don't have to work the next day, so they all come directly after work or right after picking up their other kids from school, and everyone stays longer. The healthy kids don't have to be put in bed for school the next day, so parents drag them here rather than hire a babysitter. Tonight, we got 45 kids through here. On a weeknight we average 20. Give or take. Plus, it's extremely hard to get volunteers here on a Friday. Especially teen ones like you and Landi. Volunteering Friday nights puts a severe cramp in your social life. It's a tough sale. I was always surprised and grateful for the time Landi spent here every Friday. She was so faithful. So, committed. She was, in fact, the only volunteer I could count on to be here every Friday night."

Grandma Daisy lapsed into a silent reverie. Jazz felt the familiar spurt of anguish at those words.

"I know," Jazz said softly, facing away from the older lady. "I, well, I always wanted her to blow off coming, and she never would. It used to drive me crazy."

Grandma Daisy chuckled. "Don't feel bad about it. It's only natural. When I was your age, I wouldn't be caught dead being anywhere but out and about on a Friday night."

Jazz raised her head and looked up at Grandma Daisy. Both eyebrows raised this time.

"Hey, I wasn't always old! I knew how to have fun in my day. Not to mention I was hot looking in my day. I always had me a date on weekend nights."

Jazz smiled at the older woman. She slowly got to her feet, "Well, I think you are beautiful now."

"Girl, hush," Grandma Daisy said with a dismissive wave of her hand.

"Okay, well, I'm going home now. See you tomorrow."

"Home? Not even my girl Landi went straight home after volunteering. She was rushing off to somewhere."

Jazz nodded. She'd always made sure that something planned for Fridays. Before.

"Well, since I promised Marin I would be here bright and early tomorrow, I better go home and rest. Um, what time do we open, anyway?"

"7:30 a.m."

"What!"

Grandma Daisy chuckled. "And I believe I heard Miss Marin ask her parents what time her brother's tests were scheduled for as they were leaving."

"Please tell me 9."

"I could tell you 9. It'd be a falsehood, but I'd be happy to lie to you if you'd like and not tell you that her parents will be here bright and early at 7:30. If you get here by 7:15, the doors will be open, and someone will be here to set up check-in."

Jazz groaned.

Grandma Daisy put her arms around her and gave her a squeeze. "Oh, sweetie, you'll be fine. Early mornings ain't never killed nobody."

With a sigh, Jazz gathered her things and started toward the door. "Well, I guess I'll see you first thing tomorrow morning then."

"Oh, child, please. I'm retired. I won't be here that early. I've earned the right to sleep in. I might come wandering in here 'round 10 or so."

"What! Wait! Well, then who?"

Grandma Daisy smiled and gave her a gentle pat on the arm. "I'm afraid it will be you and Ms. Reeves opening tomorrow."

Then the older woman burst into a gale of cheerful giggles at the aghast look that appeared on Jazz's face.

All Jazz could do was groan.

CHAPTER FIFTEEN
SMELLS LIKE MEMORIES

For the first time since the accident, Jazz fell asleep
without the tossing and turning that had been plaguing
her. This was something for which she was very grateful.
That night there was no reliving the accident over and
over in her mind. No sick to the stomach feeling making
her roll this way and that as she compiled a long list of
"what ifs" and "if onlys" in her head.

Unfortunately, when her alarm woke her at 6:00 a.m.
Saturday morning, she immediately burst into tears–
something she'd done every morning since the accident.
Jazz was surprised and distressed because she'd assumed
that after all the volunteering she'd done the night before,
the overwhelming feelings of guilt and heartache she felt
every waking minute would have abated, at least a little.
After all, she'd done something positive and useful,
something for someone other than herself, something that
kept her from thinking about the accident every single
second. And most importantly, she'd done it in the

memory of Landi. Yet, as the early morning light crept through the slit in her curtains, the only thing she wanted to do was to lie in bed and sob. The familiar heavy, thick feeling of guilt and helplessness lay over her, no different from the past seven mornings. The shame weighing her down, threatening to suffocate her.

Jazz curled into a fetal position and let the tears trickle out of her eyes. She felt them change from warm to cool as they traveled down her cheek and off her chin. How could she have promised that little girl that she would return to the SibSanc this morning? If she were to be brutally honest with herself, it was clear that she wasn't the type of person a young girl like Marin needed around her. Marin needed someone like Landi. Landi would have known what to say to those kids last night who felt unimportant and forgotten. Landi wouldn't have sat there like a bump on a log, silent and dumb as a post, while surrounded by pre-teens who clearly needed words of comfort and wisdom. Landi would have told them it was okay to want their parent's attention. That it was understandable to be jealous of their sick siblings and the time the family spent focused on them. Landi would have said it only made sense to feel guilty for being able to run and bike and play soccer while their siblings were stuck in the hospital, lying in bed. Landi would have told them that their parents loved them just as much as they loved their sick kids, even if they were too stressed out and worried to show it. But instead of being smart and uplifting and helpful and kind like Landi would have been, all Jazz thought of to do was hand out tissues. Lame. Absolutely, positively pathetic.

TRACI L. JONES 121

The longer Jazz lay buried under her covers thinking about how much better a person Landi was, the more she missed her. And how stupid she was to think that one measly night of volunteering would wipe away her grief.

It was like an ache deep within her, a painful gnawing in the pit of her stomach, a tightening and compressing of her heart. It was almost unbearable. Jazz remembered one of the boys' last night quietly confessing that sometimes he wished he'd been born the sick one rather than his brother. Then he would get all the attention; all the family's focus would be on him. When he said that, Jazz suddenly realized that she harbored a similar wish. She wished she'd been the one killed. That way Landi, would be the one left alive to live alone. Landi would be the one trying to cobble together a normal life without the best friend that knew everything about you. Landi would be the one forced to lie to everyone and say she was healing as well on the inside as her cuts and bruises were healing on the outside. Jazz was sure that Landi would've been able to do it without feeling a constant nagging pain in her heart, without being continually soul-sick, without feeling lost and unhinged. Landi was the one who possessed the strength of character to ignore the suffocating feelings of guilt and sadness. Landi had the intestinal fortitude to move on with life, whereas Jazz was certain, dead certain, that she was utterly and absolutely incapable of doing any of those things. Jazz couldn't figure out how she was going to get out of bed today, much less how to live through next week, next month, or next year. Jazz was hanging on by a single, very thin, mental string.

This past summer, Jazz's biggest dilemma had been a bad hairstyle. Now, her problem wasn't a bad haircut that would eventually go away with time. It was much worse. Landi was gone forever, and it would be Jazz's fault, forever and for always.

Wallowing in the depths of her misery, Jazz would have been content to stay buried underneath her covers for all of eternity, and she would have too if it hadn't been for a familiar scent that came wafting into her room from the kitchen.

She sat bolt upright in her bed, took a deep breath, and immediately rage replaced the stifling grief she'd felt. She tossed the covers violently off her body.

"You've got to be fucking kidding me," she seethed through clenched teeth. She bounded out of bed, threw her door open with a bang, stomped down the stairs, and stormed into the kitchen.

Arms akimbo, she stood and looked around the kitchen, her anger growing exponentially by the minute. A moment of silence passed while she glared at her father, who was standing at the sink, his back towards her, gazing wistfully out of the kitchen window.

"What the hell, Dad?" she yelled at him, waving a hand at the plate of food sitting untouched on the counter.

Startled, her father jumped, spun around, wiping some tears off his face.

"Oh, God!" he moaned. "Jazz. I'm sorry!"

As she watched, he leaped into action and began throwing the stacks of pancakes into the trash, shoving the plates into the dishwasher, dumping the remaining batter down the drain.

"Oh baby, I, it's...."

"Jesus, Dad, pancakes? Seriously?" Jazz stood at the door, tears streaming down her face. "Why, Dad?"

"Honey, it's that I forgot. I woke up, went for my run, came in, and automatically started making them. I, it's, I mean," her father stammered. "I was on autopilot. Oh, baby. I forgot. I'm so sorry!"

He reached out and pulled her into a hug.

Stupid freaking pancakes.

Most Friday nights, Landi slept over at Jazz's. It started in junior high when both girls started filling out, getting boobs and curvy hips, changing from cute but irritating little girls to pretty, shapely teenagers. With five older brothers, Landi's house was always, always, filled with a gang of teenage boys. It was guaranteed that the Lewis's house would have at least six boys hanging out and sleeping over on a typical Friday night. Six hormonal teenage boys, if not seven, eight or nine of them—too many for either the Lewis's or the Sanders to feel comfortable having their pre-teen, then teen girls flouncing around in their cute little sleep shorts and tops. So once the girls hit puberty and began showing as much interest in the boys, as the boys were showing in them, their parents got together and decided, much to Landi's delight and Jazz's chagrin, that Friday nights Landi would have a standing invitation for a sleepover at Jazz's. Jazz knew that Landi loved the arrangement, as did Jazz, even with the irritating lack of fine boys at her house.

Landi found Jazz's house quieter, cleaner, and less smelly than her own. While Jazz admitted that this was indeed the case, it was also true that her house was way more boring. Landi's house was messy, loud, and chaotic. It was also fun—full of noise, excitement, and, most importantly, older teenage boys. In other words, Jazz thought Landi's house was paradise, while Landi found it tiresome, even with the house's abundance of cute boys. Of course, Landi was related to many of the cutest ones, a fact which Jazz blamed for Landi's lack of enthusiasm for staying home. Boys or no boys, Landi preferred the atmosphere at Jazz's home to the boy-filled Lewis abode.

Since Jazz was an only child, she got a ton of attention from her parents, attention which she was more than willing to share with Landi. Over time, Jazz's parents eventually began treating Landi like another daughter. And honestly, sometimes Jazz thought that maybe her father liked Landi a little better than he liked her. Not loved Landi more. Jazz was sure that her father loved her more than anyone but that he liked Landi more. With all those boys around her house, Landi was a bit of a tomboy. She loved sports, and Jazz often lost Landi to some game on television that her father was watching. One minute she and her best friend would prepare to watch some chick flick up in Jazz's room, and the next thing Jazz knew, Landi would be in the family room watching some Big Twelve football game with her dad. Before long, the three of them would be sitting on the couch screaming like maniacs.

Plus, Jazz's father had gotten a kick out of the fact that no matter what he cooked, Landi always wanted a taste, and more often than not, a plateful, of what he liked to call his "culinary experiments." Whether it was fried gizzards, Maid-rite sandwiches (which both Landi and

Jazz's dad loved, although it was just a bunch of loose hamburger meat falling off a bun), or, ugh, chitlins. Landi was always game to eat her dad's food. The same food that Jazz usually turned up her nose.

In the middle of eighth grade, Jazz's father discovered Landi's love of pancakes. Apparently, with five older brothers, getting enough to eat period was a task in and of itself, but the Lewis family all loved pancakes, and there were never enough for the baby girl of the family to eat her fill. So, every Saturday morning for the past few years, Jazz's father got up, would go for his run, and then returned to make pancakes for the girls. Well, in truth, for Landi, because Jazz was not a big pancake fan. She preferred waffles.

So here he was, after his run, a week after Landi had died, in the kitchen making freakin' pancakes. Smelling up the entire house with that stupid pancakey smell.

Jazz, whose initial fury had evaporated the minute she saw her father's tear-streaked face, stood sobbing against his chest, feeling sorry for screaming at him like a crazed banshee. This entire week she'd been so wrapped up in how she felt and how this was affecting her and her life that she hadn't given a thought about how Landi's death would impact her parents' lives, too. Landi was a fixture around their house for seven years. It must be like losing a child for her parents too—if not a child, then at least a cherished niece.

"I'm sorry I yelled Daddy," muttered Jazz. "I guess I freaked out a little."

"It's okay, baby. Although your language was unnecessary, the freaking out is not unexpected."

"What language? I only said hell."

"It's a four-letter word, Jazzlyn."

Jazz sighed, too sad and feeling too worn out to argue with her usual vigor. "I apologize."

Her father held her arm's length away. "I apologize too. I don't know what I was doing. I was on autopilot. I came in and immediately started the pancakes. I was looking for blueberries when I realized only Landi likes blueberry pancakes. Then I remembered that Landi's not here. Before the blueberries, I was actually thinking about how I was going to harass her about the Duke game coming on today."

His voice caught, and he paused. "Landi isn't here to eat my pancakes, and she's not here to argue about who's going to win today's game," he smiled down at Jazz. "I guess I hadn't realized how used to having her around I was."

Jazz nodded. She didn't trust herself to speak.

"That kid, she was over here so much... Oh, baby."

He gently wiped the tears off Jazz's face and pulled her close again. "It will get better, I promise for all of us. I was about to clean up my mess when you came in and started yelling at me. I figured it'd be at least another hour before you got up. In fact, what are you doing up so early, anyway? Couldn't sleep?"

Jazz took a deep breath and steadied herself before pulling away from the warmth and comfort of her father's embrace. She could tell that he wanted to steer the conversation away from Landi. She did too, but it seemed that all words, and all roads, lead right back to Landi.

"I'm heading to the Children's Hospital. I volunteered there last night, and I promised a little girl I'd be back for a little while today."

The look of pure shock that appeared on her father's face insulted Jazz. He raised his eyebrows but said nothing. Jazz made a face at him. She watched with confusion as the look on his face morphed from surprise to outright amusement. She frowned as an idea of what he found so funny occurred to her.

"Whatever, Dad."

"What? I didn't say anything!"

She made a W with her hands and flashed it at him before turning to head out of the kitchen.

"Wait! Landi told me she'd get you there before long, is all," he said. She could hear the withheld laughter in his voice. "She said she'd have you there by the end of the month."

Jazz stopped in her tracks and turned back towards her dad.

"She said what?"

"That she was wearing you down, and you'd be volunteering there soon. She said, 'I'm wearing her down, Colonel. It won't be long now.' That girl was too much. She knew how to handle you."

Apparently, the look on her face was comical because her father burst out laughing.

"What is so funny, Dad?"

"Oh, nothing."

"Whatever, Dad," repeated Jazz.

Her father grinned at her.

As she left the kitchen, she heard her father mutter to himself, "That Landi was something else. God love her. She was something else."

•   •

Jazz hurried through the doors of the SibSanc and stopped short. The smell almost drove her back out of the doors.

"You have got to be kidding me!" she moaned.

"Jazz!" shouted Marin. The little girl popped out of her seat in the art center and came running towards her. "Come on, Jazz! We're eating breakfast! We've got pancakes!"

Jazz bent down and gave Marin a hug.

"Good morning Marin."

"We've got pancakes!"

"Yes," muttered Jazz. "I'm being haunted by hotcakes today."

"Huh?"

"I'm followed by flapjacks."

Marin's brow crinkled. "What?"

"Nothing."

"Come on, sit by me."

Jazz allowed herself to be towed by the little girl to the arts and crafts tables, now covered with bright red plastic tablecloths. Three kids were seated eating breakfast, clearly enjoying their food.

"Have a pancake, Jazz," said Marin, shoving a plate into her hands and pointing to the stack of pancakes in the center of the table.

"Marin, my love, I am not a fan of the flapjack."

"Huh?"

"I don't like pancakes," explained Jazz. "In fact, I like them less and less as this morning progresses."

Still, she grabbed a couple of slices of bacon and a container of yogurt. "I would, however, be honored to have breakfast with you."

Marin beamed at her with a face covered in syrup.

An hour or so later, Jazz was becoming concerned that she'd turned a sweet little girl into an Uno card shark. Marin had beaten her and anyone else who dared to play against her in every single game. It was unreal.

"You know what, little girl?" whined Jazz after being left with only one Uno card in her hand when Marin won yet again. "I'm beginning to think you might have hustled me. Are you sure you didn't know how to play this game before last night?"

Marin giggled, "I can't help if I'm good at it."

"Yeah, well, I'm afraid I'm going to have to let you beat me only one more time, then I have to go home and get ready to cheer at a soccer game."

Marin pouted.

"Whoa, no pouting."

Marin frowned at her.

"Um, no frowning either."

Marin continued to frown and then suddenly smiled, "Oh yeah, Mommy said we are going to get our nails done when Mason's tests are finished. Okay, you can go."

"Thank you, ma'am. I appreciate you allowing me..."

She stopped talking as a thought came from out of nowhere, a thought so startling that it cut her voice off mid-sentence.

Manicures. Today was Saturday, and Landi is, was a creature of habit. Just like she ate pancakes every Saturday morning with Jazz and her father, she always got her nails done every Saturday with her mother. When Landi finally stopped biting her nails, sometime near the end of sixth grade, Landi and her mother had created a standing date, and in typical Landi fashion, very little could alter her from her set schedule. Jazz was sure that Landi got her structured ways from Mrs. Lewis, and now, thanks to Marin, Jazz knew what she needed to do before she made her way to the soccer game.

After being beaten again, Jazz gave Marin a final squeeze and left the little girl shuffling the cards like a Vegas dealer, grinning somewhat maniacally at her next victim.

"Bye, Marin. And thanks!"

CHAPTER SIXTEEN
NAILED TO THE WALL

Jazz pulled up to the Lewis's house and hurried out of the car. She didn't know if she had gotten there in time, but with luck, Mrs. Lewis hadn't left yet for the nail shop.

Taking the porch steps two at a time, she was about to open the door in her usual fashion when it swung open.

"What the hell are you doing here?"

Jazz's mouth dropped open. In the doorway stood her favorite Lewis brother, Linwood Lewis, Linny to everyone who knew him. Linny was the brother closest in age to Landi, and the one, at least in Jazz's opinion, who was the finest of all the Lewis boys. And all Lewis boys were beautiful, exquisite male specimens. Tall, chocolate brown, broad shoulders, big brown eyes, killer cheekbones, big, beautiful smiles. It was as if the more boys Mr. and Mrs. Lewis gave birth to, the better looking they got. Landi had been extremely pretty, but the Lewis boys were to die for—all five of them. But in Jazz's opinion, Linny was by far the hottest.

Like any normal girl presented with such male yumminess, there was no other option for Jazz but to have a crush on Linny. Starting from the minute she'd first walked into the Lewis house with Landi and saw Linny and his four older brothers sitting at the kitchen table, eating their way through an entire box of cereal and a gallon of milk. Jazz had been smitten. The other Lewis boys were big and old and slightly intimidating, especially to Jazz, a lonely, only child, but Linny had seemed accessible.

When she and Landi interrupted their mid-morning snack that first day, Landi's older brothers merely glanced up briefly before returning to their bowls, uninterested in the two young girls standing in the doorway. They were far too busy eating to pay much attention to their 10-year-old sister and her girlfriend. However, Linny, who was 12, looked up, stared right at Jazz, and presented her with a big smile—a big, beautiful, irresistible Kool-Aid grin which melted her heart immediately. From that very second, Jazz's private dream was to marry Linny and become not just an honorary Lewis, but a real, full-fledged legal member of her best friend's family.

And now, here he was standing at the Lewis's doorway, glaring at her with so much fury and anger in his eyes that it felt like a physical blow. Jazz took an involuntary step backward, trying to put some distance between the waves of animosity she felt emanating from Linny.

"Hey, Linny," she mumbled. "How are you?"

"I asked what you wanted."

Jazz's mouth opened, but she stayed silent, completely nonplussed by his reaction to her. In all the years she'd known Linny, she couldn't remember him ever being angry. Irritated maybe, particularly when he arrived home to find most of the food eaten by his older brothers. Annoyed? Sure, especially when he caught Landi and Jazz spying on him and his girlfriend. Peeved, exasperated, upset, bothered, frustrated, yes to all those, but never, not once, in the past 7 years had she ever seen him enraged. In short, he was a freaking ray of sunshine in human form—a really smoking hot, muscularly male form. Now, though, it was clear by his tense body language, the grim set of his face, the blackness of his eyes, that Linny was beyond incensed. He was livid—at her. She'd even go far as to say that he hated her; the wrath she saw in him was that intense.

"It's that I, I," stammered Jazz, completely thrown off by his reaction. "Um, are you okay?"

Linny gave a snort of derision and rolled his eyes.

"Am I okay?" he spat out. "Well, let's see. My one and only sister is dead, my mother has been crying her eyes out all morning, my dad is a zombie, and the person responsible for causing all of our misery is standing on my porch asking me if I'm all right like a simpering, stupid idiot. Shit. Hmm, I'd have to say no! Hell, no, I am not okay!"

Jazz felt as if someone had punched her in the stomach. She gasped, and her eyes filled with tears.

"Oh, this is priceless. You're crying? Are you seriously standing on my front porch crying?" As Jazz swiped away the tears, Linny's face vacillated between anger and disbelief. She took another step away.

He rolled his eyes again, muttering to himself, "You have got to be kidding me. She's fucking crying. Unbelievable. Ain't this some bullshit."

"Linny, I didn't...." Jazz explained, but he waved her quiet.

"I don't want to hear it, Jazz. Everyone gives you a pass. Well, I'm not. I know what goes on up at the Wash." Linny glared at her a moment before continuing. "Personally, I'm waiting for the police investigator to finish his report. Once everyone knows you were drinking and driving, or driving and texting, or whatever equally stupid thing you were doing instead of driving carefully, then maybe you'll get what you deserve. Maybe then everyone will stop saying how sorry they feel for you. Maybe then they stop talking about poor Jazz this, and poor Jazz that, and they'll finally start focusing on the real victim, Landi. My sister. The girl who died. You remember her, don't you? The person you killed?"

Investigation? There was an investigation taking place? Of course, there was. How could she have been so dumb to think that one wouldn't be happening? Teenagers, car crash, death. It was weird how much she could remember and how much she could forget about one night.

Some were crystal clear. Others foggy and dreamlike. Everything right up to the crash she could remember. Everything. But no matter how hard she tried, she could barely remember anything else. Who drove her away from the accident? What did the doctors ask? Her parents arriving at the hospital. It was like a black space.

A sudden chill came over her body and she shivered. What would the report show? She ignored the sudden rush of fear that flooded her body and the explosion of questions that popped into her head and tried to remain calm. She needed to stay composed, so she could make Linny understand what had happened that night.

"Linny, I wasn't, I didn't... It's not what you think!"

Linny folded his arms and shot her a nasty look. "Oh, I'm sure it's exactly what I think. Everyone else may believe you, but Malachi has a friend in the district attorney's office who is making the police department hurry up with those results. The sooner you're exposed for who you are and what you did, the better!"

Malachi, Landi's eldest brother, was an attorney with the District Attorney's office. He was so much older than she was that she didn't know much about him, except that he was crazy about his baby sister.

Jazz shook her head furiously, "I wasn't drunk, Linny. You know Landi and I don't drink! I mean not very often, and never very much! You know that!"

"Yeah, so you say," Linny sneered angrily. "There's a first time for everything. I know exactly what happens at the Wash parties. Drinking. Edibles. Getting high. All that crap. There's no reason to go if you don't drink. The whole point of the Wash is scoring free beer and drinking as much of it as you can! Getting wasted."

"We only went, well, see, we didn't even... it was, I mean," stuttered Jazz. With all the buzzing that was going on in her head, she couldn't form a complete thought, much less a complete sentence. She took another step down from the porch, hoping more distance would help clear her head. She took a deep breath and started again, "I only wanted to go...."

Linny interrupted her with a mean snort of laughter. "Oh, I already figured out that you guys went because you wanted to go, not Landi. I'm sure you dragged her with you whether or not she wanted to go. God, look at you! There's barely a mark on you—hardly a cut or a bruise. Not even a damn scratch! It's fucking amazing. No, wait, it's not so amazing. The drunks are always the ones who aren't hurt in crashes. So naturally, you haven't got a scratch on you."

Linny was yelling at her now, causing Jazz to cringe away from his voice and his accusations. "And tell me this," he continued at the top of his voice. "How is it that you had your seatbelt on and Landi didn't?"

Jazz looked down at her tennis shoes, reluctant to answer. How could she possibly explain that she hadn't meant to knock the phone from Landi's hand? What words could she put together to explain? If there was a sentence that would stop Linny from yelling, her brain couldn't come up with it. There was an awkward silence while Jazz continued to stand, head bowed, watching her tears make tiny wet circles on the pavement as they dropped from her eyes, her mind working frantically to come up with an answer that wouldn't make Linny hate her more.

As the silence extended, she could hear Linny standing at the top of the stairs huffing and puffing as if he'd recently finished running a race. Out of the corner of her eye, Jazz could see him clenching and unclenching his hands. She shivered again. She'd never seen him so agitated. Her stomach began to roil, and she clenched her teeth, willing her breakfast to stay in her stomach. At that moment, the thing she wanted more than anything else in the world was to trade places with Landi.

"Well?" Linny finally asked. "Why was she unbuckled?"

The only answer Jazz could muster up was a pathetic shrug of her shoulders. She looked up at Linny but quickly averted her eyes away from his glare.

"Yeah, whatever. Anyway, I can't imagine why you felt the need to come here, Jazz," Linny said, spitting out her name as if saying it gave his mouth a bad taste. "But I can tell you this, you are not welcome here anymore. Get the hell off my porch."

Those words were like a shove, and Jazz quickly stepped off the last porch step and was hurrying away when she heard another voice say, "Stop right there, Jazz Lynn." Jazz stopped, spun around, and saw Mrs. Lewis standing, arms crossed, in the doorway. Mrs. Lewis was glaring at Linny, who was glowering right back at her. "Linwood, unless something's changed, you don't pay a single bill around here. And until you do, don't start thinking you can dictate who is welcome here and who isn't." Mrs. Lewis said in a steely voice. "Jazz will always be welcome here, Linny." She beckoned Jazz back to the house, looking at her youngest son as if daring him to say a word. "Get back up here, Jazzy. Now, please."

Jazz shot a glance at Linny. The last thing she wanted to do was close the distance she'd put in between herself and his anger, but she knew not doing what Mrs. Lewis asked wasn't an option. All it took was one look at Mrs. Lewis's face to see that what Linny had said about his mother was true. She'd obviously spent much of the morning crying. The usually made up, well-groomed woman looked tired and sad; her eyes were swollen and red, and her face make-up free.

"You will always be welcome here, Jazzy," Mrs. Lewis said, pulling Jazz into a hug. "Always. As long as I am living, you are free to come and go. Just like you did a week ago. You were like a daughter to me before the accident, and that feeling hasn't changed."

"Jesus, Mom, she killed Landi!" burst out Linny, obviously outraged and unable to hold his tongue any longer. His words were like a dagger to her heart, and Jazz felt her knees go weak. Mrs. Lewis's arms tightened around her, giving her the physical and emotional support she needed, but didn't deserve.

"Landi is dead because of her. She shouldn't be here!"

"Boy, you are out of line," answered Mrs. Lewis. "You think Jazz summoned that herd of deer? I suggest you hush. Now."

She was speaking calmly, but Jazz heard the warning coloring her voice, and she was sure Linny did too because it was evident in his face. He clamped his mouth together, biting his tongue and probably feeling as though he'd have to bite it completely off in order to comply with his mother's wishes. Linny saw that Jazz was watching him and scowled at her. She glanced away and focused on keeping her eyes on Mrs. Lewis.

"Linny, it was an accident," Mrs. Lewis said, her voice catching. "Accidents happen all the time, baby. And yes, I know that Landi didn't have her seatbelt fastened, for who knows what reason. I could spend the rest of my life wondering why, or I can let it go and thank God that Jazz had hers buckled. Landi's seatbelt was not Jazz's responsibility. It was Landi's. Furthermore, Jazz didn't go looking for those deer and aim for them."

"But Mom," protested Linny, his voice strained. "Why didn't Landi have her seatbelt on? She always put it on!" He threw his hands up in frustration before saying, "And even if they weren't drinking like she claims, then why-"

"Linwood Prentiss Lewis!" interrupted Mrs. Lewis. "First of all, just because you are taking forensics this semester doesn't mean you know everything. Secondly, I know neither of them were drinking because they did a tox screen at the hospital that night. Both tested clean. 0% alcohol in their systems. Zero. They told us that in the ER. Made sure the police knew it immediately."

Jazz nodded earnestly, but Linny wouldn't look her way. Mrs. Lewis smirked suddenly and said, "Frankly, I think both swore off drinking the night you came home from the Wash reeking of booze and then proceeded to vomit all over my kitchen floor, as well as on their shoes. I believe that was in your junior year as well when that little mishap occurred. And, if I recall correctly," her voice rising with emotion, "You were the one driving that night. You could have easily injured yourself or someone else. And here you are, acting self-righteous and smug. Casting judgment as if you are free from mistakes. Boy, you need to calm down and be quiet. Up here acting all high and mighty like the Good Lord himself."

Linny bit his lip guiltily and began studying his fingernails. Jazz watched Mrs. Lewis's face soften again as she reached over and cupped Linny's face, raising it up and looking into his watery eyes. She breathed a deep sigh before continuing in a quieter tone, "You made it home safely by the grace of God. That's the way life is, Linny. You did everything wrong that night and lived. Landi did one thing wrong last week and died."

Mrs. Lewis opened her mouth to say more, but all that came out was a strangled sob.

Jazz chanced another look at Linny's face. He was still avoiding her eyes. Of course, being ignored by him was better than being subjected to the looks she'd been getting from him a minute ago. When she saw tears running down his cheeks, she felt her heart catch; Linny crying upset her even more than Linny angry.

The three of them were silent for a minute, and then Mrs. Lewis stifled a sob, cleared her throat, and said, "I know how much you miss your sister. I know how close you were. I would say that she was one of your best friends, closer and more dear to you than any of your brothers. I saw how much you two loved each other. We all miss her. As does Jazz."

"I know you are angry and upset," Mrs. Lewis paused here, took a deep breath, drew herself up, and pinned Linny down with a steady gaze. "But, Linwood, you will not blame Jazz for her death. Don't you dare think the pain you feel gives you the right to cast judgment, assign blame, or grants you the privilege to say such mean and hurtful things to someone who your sister loved. Someone who all of us love. I will not have you stand there and treat Jazz like some stranger who did harm to your sister on purpose. I love you, but you are nowhere near perfect. Accidents happen. Kids make mistakes. In fact, we as parents expect our children to make mistakes. Sometimes that's the only way they can learn some of life's lessons. And too often, all we can do as parents is stand by, watch you guys screw up, and hope and pray that you live through the mistakes you make and learn from them."

"But Mom, Jazz was driving," Linny repeated, his voice quivering under the weight of his emotion, making him sound 8 instead of 18. Mrs. Lewis let go of Jazz and pulled her youngest son close.

"Yes, Jazz was driving. And Landi was riding without a seat belt, and the deer were crossing the street," said Mrs. Lewis, her voice cracking. Jazz closed her eyes and willed herself to hold in the gut-wrenching sobs that were building inside her. "And sometimes life sucks."

"Well, the investigation may show-" started Linny.

"It doesn't matter what the investigation shows, Linny," said Mrs. Lewis tiredly. "Landi is gone. A police report won't change that."

"Yeah, well, she may not have been drinking, but I bet she was texting and not watching the road," insisted Linny.

Unable to stay quiet, Jazz interjected, "It was, well, I mean, it wasn't me who -"

"Jazz, hush baby," interrupted Mrs. Lewis. "This conversation is over. Do you hear me, Linwood? Over."

The two Lewises stared at each other for a moment. Jazz desperately wanted to be somewhere else. She began studying her shoes again.

"Did you need something, Jazzy, or were you just coming by to say hi?"

"Huh?" Jazz looked up, careful to avoid even a quick glance in Linny's direction. "I mean, excuse me?"

Mrs. Lewis gave her fleeting smile before repeating, "Did you come by for a specific reason? Was there something you needed?"

"Well, it was that I know that you and-" Jazz stopped short and shot a furtive look over at Linny. He raised an eyebrow at her, crossed his arms, and leaned against the doorway. She swallowed and continued, "I know that you usually go and get your nails done on Sat-"

Linny snorted again and let out an exasperated sigh before muttering something under his breath. Jazz concentrated on not looking in his direction. "I thought maybe I could, I mean, we could go- "

"Mom and I are going to lunch and a movie," interrupted Linny. "She doesn't need to go anywhere with you."

Mrs. Lewis frowned and turned to Linny. "Linwood, I asked you to empty the trash in the kitchen for me. Have you done so?"

Linny frowned at his mother, who crossed her arms and looked at him without blinking. He fixed his face into a less angry look for her but shot Jazz one last hate-filled glare before disappearing into the house.

Once he was gone, Jazz let loose the sobs she'd been straining to hold in.

"Oh sweetie," Mrs. Lewis said softly, pulling Jazz in for another hug. "He's taking it so hard. He doesn't mean all those nasty things he said."

Jazz continued to sob, unable to control herself enough to say anything.

"Hey, hey, look at me," Mrs. Lewis said, holding Jazz arm's length away. "Jazzy, chin up, eyes front. Listen and hear me. I don't care if you and Landi were three sheets to the wind, falling down drunk. I don't care if you'd been driving the car with your feet while you were texting. What happened happened because God had planned it from the beginning. From the moment he put Landi Renee into my stomach, God knew she'd only be here for 17 short years. I don't know why God gave me a baby girl I wanted so bad only to take her away, but I have to concentrate on thanking him for giving her to me at all. I prayed so hard for a girl, and he finally gave me one. I guess I should have been a little more specific in my request is all."

Mrs. Lewis smiled. Jazz did her very best to return it.

"I know that you loved Landi like a sister, and you would never ever do anything to hurt her if you could have possibly helped it. Linny, well, he..." she paused and smiled another quick smile before continuing. "Linny has never been angry a day in his life. It's been easy for him from day one. He doesn't know how to handle this much pain and sorrow. He's been stomping around, being nasty, and snapping at every one since Saturday. He has had no practice with feeling such profound grief and sadness. Plus, I think it surprised him how fiercely he loved Landi and how intensely he misses her. Did you know they talked at least once a day? Not to mention the constant texts they sent back and forth. He took her cell phone. I imagine so he can always read their conversations."

Mrs. Lewis paused and blinked several times. Jazz simply let the tears fall.

"Jazz, please remember that this will be a huge adjustment for Linny. For us all, you included. But, if you can find it in your heart, please try to forgive him for everything he said. He needs someone to blame."

"Of course, I'll forgive him," Jazz said while hoping that Linny would someday forgive her because the reality was that she was to blame. "But the investigation will-"

Mrs. Lewis shook her head sadly. "Put all that stuff out of your head, Jazzy. I won't lie to you. There are family members who will always blame you for Landi's death. Linny clearly does, and so does Malachi. But the rest of us, Mr. Lewis, Micah, Lamont, and Maddox, we all look at it differently." She gave Jazz's shoulders a squeeze. She shrugged and said softly, "God giveth and God taketh away. Or in other words, life sometimes bites. All I can do is pray for acceptance of his will."

Mrs. Lewis's hand slid down Jazz's shoulders to her hands. They stood holding hands a minute before Mrs. Lewis gave her hands a squeeze. "So what time does the game start?"

"Huh?"

A chuckle escaped from the older woman before she waved her hand up and down at Jazz, "Well unless you are wearing your cheerleading uniform for the heck of it, I'm assuming you are heading to a game."

Jazz gave her head a little shake. She had totally forgotten about the soccer game in her rush to get to the Lewis' before Mrs. Lewis left.

"Oh, not until 3:00. I thought we'd have time to, you know, get at least a manicure."

"That's sweet. I appreciate it, Jazz. I really do, but as my evil youngest son said before taking his funky behind inside, we are going to do lunch and a movie. It's probably best for both of us to create some new habits and routines. Why don't you run on home, grab something to eat, and rest a little before the game? Come back and see me next week, though. I'm dying to know how the volunteering at the hospital went!"

Jazz nodded and forced a smile. "Yes, ma'am, I will." She felt her eyes shift from the older lady's face to the hallway beyond the front door.

"Don't you think too much on Linny. I'll talk to him."

Jazz smiled feebly again, "Okay. But the police will-"

"Don't you worry a bit about that investigation, either! You hear me, gal? Tell me you won't spend another minute thinking about it. Do you promise me?"

Jazz forced her head to move up and down but knew that her nod was a lie even as she was doing it.

CHAPTER SEVENTEEN
WHO'S WINNING?

If someone would've asked Jazz what the score of the soccer game was, even two seconds after it ended, she could not have told them. She didn't even know whether her team won or lost. The only thing she knew for certain was that she'd done a decent job of appearing normal, well, except for the time when she stood completely still and silent during at least half of one cheer. Jazz felt sure that she made it through the game, looking like the standard, normal version of the McNair High cheerleader. Well, a cheerleader with slightly puffy red eyes, anyway.

Occasionally during the duration of the game, it felt like she was having an out-of-body experience, but all in all, based on the inane and silly comments directed towards her by her fellow cheerleaders, Jazz figured she pulled off the happy cheerleader act. She'd no idea how because the entire time she was at the game clapping and jumping and cheering, she'd been on the verge of breaking. Despite her promise to Mrs. Lewis, all Jazz could think about was the police investigation into the accident. She stupidly assumed that the blood test at the hospital that night had been all that was going to happen. Clearly though, based on what Linny said this afternoon, there was still some research going on into what exactly happened that night.

Politely turning down an invitation from other members of the squad to smoothies after the game, Jazz sighed with relief when she finally got into her car and away from all the annoying happiness, the irritating carefreeness of the other girls. It was a liberating feeling to be able to stop smiling.

With nothing to do for the rest of the evening, Jazz found herself driving around aimlessly after the soccer game, thinking about what Linny said to her that afternoon. Just remembering his words gave Jazz a sick feeling in the pit of her stomach. For so long, she nursed a little girl's fantasy that she and Landi would end up being real sisters if she married Linny. Her only hope of regaining his friendship back was that he always listened to his parents. Where Landi was prone to subtle disobedience, Linny strove to always make their parents happy and proud. Maybe after a few months, he'd see the light? She thought back to the tone of his voice and the look on his face as he stood yelling at her, and something in her broke. The thought of no longer being able to even pretend that marrying Linny was a possibility, no matter how remote or fanciful, filled Jazz's eyes with so many tears that it was becoming difficult to see where she was going. She pulled over and turned her car off. Cradling the steering wheel in her arms, she sobbed.

A knock on her window startled her out of her misery, and she looked up to see that she was stopped in front of St. Anne's. Father Peter was peering through her window, his face red, sweaty, and full of concern. She wiped away her tears, rolled down her window, and attempted a smile.

"Hey, what up, Father Peter!" she said as brightly as she could

"Good evening, Jazz. Are you all right?"

"I'm fine. Well, as fine as someone who's a complete mess can be, anyway."

Jazz wiped her face again and tried to give the priest a sincere grin, but it felt like the corners of her mouth weighed a ton. Based on the disbelieving look Father Peter gave her in return, she was pretty sure that she'd given him a grimace instead of a smile. Lifting her lips required too much work, so she let them drop back into a frown. After all the playacting she'd done at the soccer game, she didn't have the energy to front anymore today.

Father Peter pulled a handkerchief from his pocket, wiped his face, and stretched, all the while looking as if he was formulating what he was going to say to her next. She could guess the subject matter, and Jazz knew that whatever it was he was trying to decide to say was going to be something she didn't want to hear. She cast around her brain, desperately trying to think of a subject to divert him from his thoughts. It was then she noticed what he was wearing. The young priest wore running pants, tennis shoes, and an old, tattered sweatshirt, under which he had on his white priest's collar. His rosary hung around his waist. And fancy white headphones circled his neck. The perfect distraction.

"Um, what exactly are you wearing?"

He chuckled a little, rather self-abashedly, before answering.

"I know it looks weird, but I need to start jogging again. My parishioners keep bringing me cakes, cookies, and pies, and it seems rude not to eat them. So, I decided I needed to do something physical to counteract the results of their generosity, but I didn't think it proper to be seen without at least part of my vestment, so I figured I'd wear at least my collar and my rosary — sort of a blend of buff and manly, and pious and priestly. Does it look too crazy?"

Jazz chuckled a bit, "Um, yeah, it looks a hot mess, but hey, I'm Baptist. What do I know? That look could be all the rage for physically fit priests all over Rome. And wait." She held up a hand. "Is that Drake coming out of your headphones?"

Father Peter laughed and fumbled with his phone. For a second, she thought she heard Cardi B before the music went silent.

"I don't even know what to say about your taste in music. I mean, is hip hop even pope sanctioned music?"

"Hey, the Pope probably can't resist a good beat either. Seems like you're getting your sense of humor back. How's it been going? I've been hoping you'd reappear. I wanted to talk to you a little more about absolution. I got the feeling you weren't understanding the whole concept, and I-"

"Oh, no worries, Father," interrupted Jazz hurriedly. "I googled it. It's all good. I have been doing some volunteer work at the Children's Hospital. I'm thinking that's a pretty good start, right? Performing acts of mercy and charity and stuff. Actually, pretty much the only time I feel halfway normal is when I'm helping out, focusing on others, you know?"

"Well, yes, Jazz. That's wonderful to hear. I do think, though, that I should explain the whole concept a bit more clearly. You see–"

"Nah, no worries," she repeated. "I got this. Thanks though. Good looking out!"

Jazz poured as much sincere cheerfulness into her voice as she could. At that moment, she didn't think she could bear another serious discussion about anything remotely connected with Landi or her guilt. She started her car and straightened her seatbelt.

"Well, it's been nice chatting with you, Father Peter, but I better be getting home. I don't want to be out too late. My parents have been pretty clingy lately."

Father Peter heaved a frustrated sigh before nodding. "I understand. Well, please know that you are always welcome back, Baptist or not." He stepped back from the car.

"Thanks, Father. I appreciate it."

Jazz waved at him as she rolled her window up. He gave her a halfhearted wave back. As she pulled away, she glanced in her rearview mirror and saw that Father Peter was watching her drive away, shaking his head slowly.

• •

Monday morning Jazz stood by her locker, willing herself not to stick her head inside of it. She knew that getting into the habit of standing with her head buried in a school locker was no way to convince people that she was mentally stable. So instead, she was standing next to the locker, opening and closing the door, breathing in the scent of the candles with each gust of scented air.

She leaned back against the wall, trying to decide how she felt about being at school. The rest of her weekend had passed quietly. Without Landi, she didn't have anyone to hang out with, so she'd spent Saturday night with her parents. At least she tried to. When she'd appeared in the family room after changing out of her cheer uniform, they'd immediately started grilling her about her day. Apparently, Mrs. Lewis had called and apologized about Linny's behavior, which naturally meant another hour of talking about the second thing in her life that she never wanted to even think about, much less talk about, ever again. That talk, of course, logically led to a discussion about the first thing in her life that she never wanted to discuss again, the accident and Landi's death.

The only good thing about this discussion was it allowed her to bring up the investigation. Unfortunately, her parents acted much the same way as Mrs. Lewis, waving away any worries she might have about what the police report might find. Claiming that they hadn't bothered to tell her about it because they knew nothing would result from it.

During the length of the discussion, Jazz realized it would have been an opportune time to confess what really happened. She sat half-listening to her parents, all the while trying to figure out how best to explain to them what occurred that night. However, nothing came to mind. The shame of it all was too much. Even though it was getting harder and harder not to say anything about the cell phone and the texting that had taken place immediately prior to the accident, Jazz didn't say a word, and the moment passed. It was pure cowardice, and she knew it, but she didn't think she could handle the change her parents would make from pitying and coddling her to being ashamed of and furious with her.

For the first time in a very long time, Jazz got out of bed Sunday morning and went to church, much to her parents' delight. And even though service had taken up a good-sized portion of the day's hours, Sunday afternoon still dragged by so slowly that by five o'clock, she'd found herself re-reading her homework assignments and wishing Monday morning would hurry up and come.

Now, Monday morning was here, and much to Jazz's displeasure, its appearance did nothing to lighten her mood. So, here it was, five minutes before first period, and she found herself at her locker, fanning the door and feeling as if a chunk of her mind, or maybe it was her heart, was missing.

"Hot?"

Jazz shook herself out of her reverie and looked up into the face of Sir Cuteness himself, Brandon.

"Well, I'm sure it's much cooler way up there where you live, but down here closer to the ground, it's pretty warm." She smiled, pleased that she'd come up with an old Jazz response. Brandon, on the other hand, stared down at her, stone-faced and unsmiling.

"So, what up with you?" she asked, feeling a tad concerned. Usually, even the silliest of comments she made got some sort of reaction.

"What up with me?" said Brandon, sounding annoyed. "What up with you? I didn't think you were the type to play games, but I guess I was wrong."

Jazz frowned, puzzled by the irritation in his voice and the scowl on his face. "Excuse me?"

"So, you can't answer your cell, or call a brother back, or what?"

Jazz furrowed her brow, trying to figure out what he meant when it suddenly dawned on her what he was talking about. She clapped a hand over her mouth in chagrin. "Oh shit! Our date."

Brandon's eyebrows shot up in surprise. "Damn, you saying you forgot about me and our plans? That is so wrong." Brandon looked at her with a mixture of surprise, hurt, and anger. "I don't think that's ever happened to me before," he added, sounding amazed. "You shitting me, right?"

Jazz would have been amused by his arrogance if she wasn't so embarrassed and stunned by her forgetfulness. Forgetting about a date with the finest boy in school was not normal.

"Dude, I'm so sorry," Jazz stammered.

"You seriously forgot about me? Even after I called and texted you?" he asked, suddenly sounding much younger than 17. "I mean, for real?"

She shook her head frantically, eager to convince him otherwise, although, in truth, she hadn't thought a single minute all weekend about Brandon or their tentative plans. It had not crossed her mind. At all. Instead, her head had been filled with, first the hospital and volunteering, then with Landi, then with Linny and his anger, then Landi again, then the investigation, then Landi, and then Linny, and then Landi, Landi, Landi. On and on and on in an endless cycle of mental misery. In the turmoil of her thoughts, Brandon and their Saturday evening date hadn't rated a single thought all weekend. Not even a fleeting one. That was not something she wanted to tell him though. She didn't think his ego could take it, for one. Besides, making him feel bad would only make her feel worse. Not something she needed right now, for sure.

"I called you like ten times," Brandon was saying. "Before I finally got the hint, anyway."

He looked around, embarrassed, and added in a lower voice. "I mean, if you want me to step off, you can say, but I kind of thought you liked me, Jazz."

"I do, Brandon," explained Jazz, matching his same soft tone. "Honest. I do." Although, in the back of her mind, there with a tiny voice saying that if she hadn't thought about Brandon since Friday afternoon when he'd given her the idea to volunteer at the hospital, then maybe she didn't like him as much as she thought she did. An even louder voice added that she didn't deserve him, anyway.

She ignored both voices. They were so not being helpful.

"You like me, but you can't be bothered to return a call or a text? I mean, if you aren't into me, fine, you know, let a brother know. That's all I'm saying."

Jazz looked up at him and was quiet for a minute, feeling a mixture of sympathy, irritation, and exasperation.

"I don't have my phone, Brandon. I haven't since, well, since, you know, that night. Landi was texting you back, not me, remember? Then she, well, the phone... I'm pretty sure that the police have it. Oh, God, they are probably reading all my texts as we speak. So, if you get a call from the police, that's why. They are still investigating the crash and me."

Jazz watched as her explanation crystallized in Brandon's head; his face morphed from irritated to dismay to pity.

"Ah damn, Jazz, my bad." Now it was his turn to slap his head. "I didn't even think... you know. Wow. That's deep. Man, the police probably think I'm some sort of stalker."

"No, no, it's my fault. I should have given you my home number Friday afternoon."

"Jazz, it didn't occur to me that the last time you had your phone was Friday night. Talk about a major brain fart. Especially since I was the last one to text you. Sorry I came at you all pissed off and stuff. Damn. That is deep. I mean, I was one of the last ones to talk to Landi. I mean text, but still. Damn."

Jazz watched as this new thought sunk into Brandon's psyche. It was as if she could almost see it become part of his life's story. He leaned up against the locker, his head tilted back, his eyes staring up at nothing.

"Shit."

She watched as he blinked quickly.

"It's fine, Brandon, really. It's all good."

God, if he started crying, she'd lose it.

"Naw, it isn't cool. Actually, it's pretty fucked up if you want to know the truth. I was so excited about... well, it's that I was looking forward to hanging with you."

His voice trailed away. He closed his eyes briefly and gave his head a little shake before saying, "I guess I never thought, you know, about the timing of stuff. Like, that's some wild shit to have to deal with. God, and you were right there. In the car, with her when she-" Brandon looked down at her, the pity still evident in his eyes. "No wonder you've been blowing me off. I must seem like a total jackass. Coming at you all hard. Damn, Jazz. We had so much fun at the Wash that night, well, before, you know... My bad. I mean, you weren't really blowing me off. It's that you ain't that person no more. How could you be?"

Jazz thought back to that night at the Wash, to the person he was talking about, the carefree, chatty, charming Jazz Sanders he was hoping to spend time with again. She was beginning to believe that happy-go-lucky, amiable girl died with Landi on the dark road. She also wondered whether she'd ever feel carefree and happy again. She wondered whether Brandon would like the person she was now.

Whoever that was. This Jazz was new to her too.

"I don't know how much fun I'd be anymore, Brandon," she admitted. "Sometimes, I don't know if I will ever feel happy or have fun again or whether I even deserve to." She stopped, swallowing the lump in her throat. Afraid to say anymore because she knew her voice would shake.

The look on Brandon's face told her she'd said too much, gone too deep for him. It was painfully clear that her last comment had made him uncomfortable. He pinched his lips together and gazed for a moment over her head. Finally, he looked down at her, "Look Jazz," he began, but before he could say anything further, the warning bell rang, and simultaneously three of his fellow basketball players appeared from around the corner, cuffing his head and jostling him like overgrown puppies.

She quickly pulled on the social mask over the true face she'd just shown Brandon and immediately played the role of the old Jazz, saying the random silly stuff that she always did, allowing her social muscle memory to take over. From the corner of her eye, she could see Brandon watching her performance. What he thought of it, she couldn't tell.

CHAPTER EIGHTEEN
BY ANY OTHER NAME

A few weeks later, Jazz sat at her usual lunch table, letting the conversations flow over and around her, only taking part often enough so that people wouldn't look askance at her for being quiet.

In her head, she was trying to calculate. Even though she hadn't intended to keep count, she knew it'd been 24 days since the accident. She was trying to figure out the time to the hour. She didn't know why. It didn't matter, but she couldn't help it. Whenever she got too relaxed, felt too good, she'd mentally pinch herself and start adding up the days, figuring out the hours, reminding herself that she deserved no peace, no bit of real enjoyment. The only reprieve from mental self-punishment was her time at the Sibling Sanctuary. There, when she was immersed in helping the kids and running around, she felt like she could allow herself to feel almost happy. She was, after all, focused on doing something for others. In this, she felt justified in the sense of well-being that volunteering brought. Outside of the sanctuary, she was on constant guard, making sure life's little pleasures stayed far away.

And Brandon had backed away a bit. With club basketball starting up, his free time was becoming limited. Out of the blue, last Friday, he'd shown up to the Sib Sanc, but it had been even crazier than usual, with barely any time to say hi to him. When she looked again, he was gone.

Part of her liked he was there on one of his rare free Fridays, looking for her. Yet another, more boisterous part of her liked the time she spent without his distracting presence. There was a deep satisfaction in working there, and she knew Landi had been right. She loved it.

She still hadn't gotten a new cell phone, which struck her as a bit ludicrous. She's gotten a car like the next day, but a cell phone? Her parents hadn't even mentioned it. Maybe they were waiting for her to say something. To ask for a new one. That would have been the old Jazz, nagging them about getting her a phone, freaked out about everything she was missing, pissed off that she'd lost all her streaks. Upset because she had posted nothing to her story in days.

But most days, she didn't even think about it. After the initial discussion with Brandon about the police having it, she'd wondered how her parents were not freaking out about not being able to track her. A few days after that, she'd found the device in her car that tracked her car. If not for spilling her trail mix, she'd probably wouldn't have seen it, but there it was, plugged into a weird hole under her steering wheel. The old Jazz would have unplugged it and thrown it out, feeling outraged at this invasion of her privacy. The new one didn't care. Let them watch her go back and forth to school, to the occasional soccer game and track meet. She was fine with having them see her go every Friday to the hospital.

This new Jazz was more of an observer than the old one. Since the accident, she'd learned a lot, not only about herself but about what her fellow students thought about her. And what they thought of Landi. Enough time had passed, for them at least, and bit by bit, they were taking off the kid gloves they'd been using on her for the few weeks, and Jazz wasn't sure if she was all that thrilled by what she was learning.

For one, it was now clear to her that she talked too much. Or at least, she used to. She didn't anymore. Now it took a conscious act for her to take part in a conversation. Only now, since it was so difficult for her to engage with others, did she realize how much she'd run off at the mouth before. Her classmates, though, seemed to assume that she was supposed to be the one creating the topics for discussion, telling the jokes, commanding everyone's attention, spouting her opinion on a variety of subjects, and driving the conversation forward. In the back of her mind, she thought that she should feel proud that she was the leader of her peers in that respect. After all, no one else seemed to be able to pull together a group of divergent people into a lively conversation like she could effortlessly do. Yet, Jazz wasn't feeling it. In fact, she now thought most of the subjects her friends talked about were inane and silly. They were still yapping about the same stuff they always had, but now those subjects no longer interested her.

It wasn't as if she wanted to talk about the meaning of life and death or any other deep crap like that. Still, she would have loved to share her experiences at the Children's Hospital with them. Get their opinion on how to help younger kids get through some of the stuff they were forced to deal with, but she instinctively knew that their eyes would quickly glaze over with disinterest—like hers whenever Landi talked about the SibSanc. She didn't blame them or even look down at them for it. Rather, she could see, and even understand, where they were coming from. Jazz knew that they hadn't changed, but she had. It was a fundamental, deep-seated change, and it wasn't something with which she was particularly happy or comfortable. A large part of her wanted desperately to care about who was dating whom or what the latest song was, but she couldn't find it in herself to care. Even a little bit. She'd lost count of the times her friends asked her why she was being so quiet, a question she felt was one of the dumbest questions ever. Everyone at this table was at Landi's memorial service, for fuck's sake! Dumb shits.

Why so quiet, Jazz? Geez. Get a clue.

Another part of her, though, thought that perhaps, in the long run, this new way of thinking, her new way of life, was something that would do her some good. For instance, she was now "so quiet" because she'd begun only saying something when she knew that it was something meaningful to say. Otherwise, she kept her mouth shut. It was completely out of character. Which was why, Jazz figured, people insisted on asking her that stupid question. Her mother often told her that just because something popped into her head, that didn't mean it needed to come out of her mouth, and for the first time, she understood what her mother was trying to teach her. Jazz got it, but her classmates didn't, and she now constantly reminded herself not to act irritated when questioned about her new reserved nature by her friends, but it was a struggle.

And speaking of friends, Jazz was beginning to think that Landi was the only true friend she had. Well, used to have anyway. Despite being surrounded by people she once thought of as "her group," Jazz was beginning to stop thinking of them as "friends." That word, friend, implied a closeness with someone—a sort of deep knowledge of another's likes, dislikes, hopes, and fears. She was stunned to discover there wasn't anyone she talked to regularly, and her so-called friend group appeared to know her barely at all. Each day brought into sharper focus how tight she and Landi were and how they'd done an unbelievable job of shutting other people out of their two-person circle, even while acting as if they were part of a big group of friends. More than once during a typical day, someone said something that caused Jazz to look to her right to give Landi a smirk, a smile, or a lift of an eyebrow. Jazz never noticed before how much of their communication used to be non-verbal—almost as if they'd shared a single brain. And weirdly, it occurred to her now that Landi always used to sit on Jazz's right side. It was those moments she missed her friend most acutely. Whenever those little, tiny things came to her attention. It was this aggravating, heartbreaking mix of little things she hadn't noticed until now that would cause her heart to ache at random times during the school day. The big things she expected to miss (although knowing she was going to miss something did nothing to lessen the sting of their absence), but it was the myriad of tiny stuff that made each day an unbelievably hard mental chore to get through.

Landi always sat or stood to her right. A little thing. Landi also-

"Yo Jazz!"

A deep male voice from the end of the table shook Jazz out of her reverie. Jazz looked up from picking half-heartedly at her lunch toward the direction of the voice.

"Yes, how can I help you?" Jazz answered, automatically assuming one of the many voices from what Landi called her "cadre of idiotic characters" and which Jazz preferred to call her repertoire of clever accents.

The voice belonged to Keyvaughnjay, who sat at the opposite end of the table, flanked as usual, by his boys, O.C. and Devin. Landi had nicknamed them The Wit Brothers after a stunningly stupid stunt they'd pulled in middle school.

"There they are," she'd said in an undertone to Jazz one day as they walked by them in the hallway. "The Wit brothers; Nit, Dim and Half."

"Yo," he repeated.

"Yes, you've said that," replied Jazz. "Are you asking me for a toy because I have no Yo-Yo with me at the moment, or did you have a complete sentence in mind?"

Keyvaughnjay smirked, "See there, Jazz, you always got something smart to say."

"Well, I try," answered Jazz breezily. "Far more impressive than always having something dumb to say, don't cha think?"

Out of habit, she glanced to her right after her witty retort, her heart plummeting to her feet at the sight of the empty space beside her.

"Yo, anyway," Keyvaughnjay repeated. "We was wondering why your girl always called us the Wit Brothers."

Uh oh.

"Well, um," Jazz stuttered, casting around her brain for a good, non-insulting answer. "Because you guys are so witty?"

She internally grimaced at the way her voice raised in tone at the end of her sentence, making it a question rather than a statement. "Yep," she added with false certainty. "That's why. She said it was because you are so witty."

Jazz pointedly ignored the faces of the other students at the table, which were either vaguely confused by her assertion, or, as in the case of Brandon, outright disbelieving. The Wit Brothers were many things, but witty was not one of them. But Jazz nodded and smiled so aggressively at them that no one said anything to challenge her remark. Thank God.

There was a moment of silence before Keyvaughnjay said, "Yeah, yeah. I get it. That's about right!" The other two boys hooted, gave each other fist bumps, and seemed satisfied. Jazz tried to hold her face straight so as not to give away the things that were going through her mind, happy to have dodged a bullet.

"Well, she used to call me Essay."

Shit.

Jazz looked down the table at Jeremy, aka Essay. Landi started calling him that when she was his lab partner freshman year. "He can't answer a simple yes or no question. Every answer that comes out of his mouth is a four-page essay."

"Huh," Jazz said. "Well…"

Think, think, think.

"It's because, she always thought, that uh," Jazz started. Out of the corner of her eye, she could see Brandon smirking. He seemed to be the only one who noticed how she was struggling.

"You see," Jazz began again. "You seemed very deep to her. Yes, because you are very deep, and you aren't simple, and you are complicated, and she, Landi, that is, she felt that you were not easy, like a multiple-choice test. You were like an essay exam, you know, more, um, more thoughtful. Get it?"

Please, just say yes, thought Jazz desperately. Just say yes, Jeremy.

"Well, you know," Jeremy said, slowly and thoughtfully. "I do believe that I understand what she meant. We often had very deep and meaningful conversations during our lab class. You know we were lab partners, both this year in science and freshman year. And I remember that she once told me that simple was not good enough for me. Landi was very perceptive, you know. I'd often thought that about her, and I think I probably knew that all along, but you know she was pretty secretive about how she came up with her nicknames. She told me once that it was one of her gifts. But thank you, Jazz, I've often wondered, and now I get it. And you know...."

"So that's a yes, then?" Jazz asked, interrupting what was bound to be another wordy dissertation. She tried to keep the smile that was playing on her lips from staying.

"Oh, you bet! I appreciate you telling me, Jazz. Like I said, I'd often wondered why she called me Essay."

"Okay, me next!" piped up Olivia.

Jazz stifled a groan.

"Although she told me once," Olivia said. "But I can't remember."

Oh, dear Lord, thought Jazz. She took a quick survey of those who were at the lunch table and figured this conversation was going to go downhill quickly.

Landi called Olivia Mahlody for some time now. It was not a nice nickname.

"Geez, look at Olivia's head," Landi had said in gym last year. "It's huge. She's like, Head-mahlody, all head, and no body."

And from then, she'd called the girl "Mahlody." Landi could be mean.

"Wait, I think I remember her saying something like it was because I was so different, but instead of marching to a different drum, I danced to a different melody, but the word melody was too boring, so she started calling me 'Mahlody.'"

"Um, yep, sure," nodded Jazz. "We'll go with that then, shall we? So, has anyone seen the new Beyoncé video? I heard she was going to go on tour next year. I wonder if she'll come here...."

No one took the bait. Jazz glanced around at the other expectant faces; Rachel "New Money" Johnson, Ricky "Pope" Sanchez, Dana and Debra aka "The Twiddle sisters," Andy Hall and Jordan Parker, "Thing 1 and Thing 2", "Red Cup" Lexy, and that was only one side of the long lunchroom table. Jazz didn't even know who knew they even had a nickname or not. Sometimes Landi's creations were so mean that she never used them in public, only in private when talking to Jazz. Some names were inside jokes that she couldn't even explain if she tried. When Alaine "Toot" Butler caught her eye and opened her mouth, it was officially time to panic, so Jazz did the only thing that made sense. She bolted.

Standing abruptly, Jazz gathered her things and snatched up her tray.

"All this talk about Landi is...." Jazz blurted out. "I gotta go."

She turned on her heel and ran out of the lunchroom.

Seconds later, Jazz was in the bathroom throwing up. When she'd run from the lunchroom, she wanted to escape from the curious, seeking eyes of her classmates, but as she hurried away, she felt the heat rising to her face; the bile rising in her throat, and she'd gotten to the bathroom in just enough time to empty the contents of her stomach into the nearest toilet.

After she was finished, Jazz sat for a moment on the seat, her face buried in her hands, cursing Landi again for making her give up her e-cig habit. Nicotine would feel pretty good right now. Anything to take the edge off or at least help remove the nasty taste in her mouth.

For the first few days after the accident, she'd thrown up quite a bit. Whenever she thought too much about Landi's death or re-lived the crash, anything that was in her stomach would reverse direction and end up back outside of her body. As the weeks progressed, though, the vomiting ceased. In fact, this was the first time since after the funeral she'd lost it. Not that lots of stuff didn't turn her stomach and make her nauseous, but she usually could swallow it down. Seeing all those faces looking at her, expecting her to explain Landi's thinking, triggered it.

What was worse was the thought that crossed her mind as she was scanning the faces of her friends, listing their various nicknames in her head. It was the sudden realization that most of Landi's nicknames for her classmates were not always focused on their most positive traits. Second, if Jazz was forced to go through the entire table, she would be sure to run out of plausible lies for some of the meaner nicknames Landi had given to some of her least favorite people. Of course, being privy to all the thought processes and reasons behind each and every nickname Landi bestowed, Jazz knew that most of them were not flattering. Yet it was the thought, "Well, Landi wasn't always a very nice person," crossing her mind, which was what sent her racing to the bathroom. That Jazz's brain even formulated such a disloyal thought about her very best friend was shocking to Jazz's system. How dare she, the one that is living, the one with no broken bones, the one whose bruises or cuts were faded and healed, have the nerve to think such a mean thing about Landi.

Landi was the one who volunteered at a hospital, the one who arranged their academic lives, the one who was on student council, the girl who organized not only a can food drive for the homeless but a toy drive for the homeless children; the girl with the 3.8 G.P.A., the president of the young adult group at church. Landi was the perfect one. Landi was the dead one.

Jazz was only the sometimes amusing sidekick. Landi was the hero, the main act, the superstar. Yet, here Jazz was, subordinate that she was, thinking unkind thoughts about her. It was enough to make anyone sick to their stomach.

Jazz felt queasy again at the thought that her own mind could betray her best friend. Maybe that little voice in her head was right. That nagging voice that told her she was unfit to be living, undeserving of any happiness and laughter. Clearly, that voice had a valid argument. After all, if she couldn't be loyal to the memory of her best friend, how could she be worthy of a guy like Brandon or of anything or anyone else good that might come along. Thank God he'd backed away a bit.

"Jazz?"

A voice called from the other side of the stall. So deep in thought, and disgust, with herself, Jazz hadn't heard the restroom door open. Straightening herself up, she opened the door to find Lyric Howard standing by the bathroom sinks, waiting for her to appear.

"You okay?"

Jazz nodded before giving a weary lift of her shoulders. "I guess. I, it's..," she closed her mouth, trying to gather her thoughts. "I guess I freaked out a little bit. Talking so much about Landi. I still can't believe she's gone."

Lyric nodded. "You guys were tight. I mean, even though you were both friends with, like, everybody, it was still just the two of you. You know. Like conjoined twins or something. For forever. Since what? Fourth grade?"

Jazz felt a rush of relief. Someone who finally got it!

"Yeah, it was fourth grade. I don't know, Lyric. It's hard. I keep waiting for it all to get easier."

A frown crossed Lyric's face, "Jazz if it gets any easier, it won't be anytime soon."

Jazz's eyes filled. She turned away and began washing her hands to give herself something to do.

"Look, if you ever want to talk or hang out or something, call me. And, um, Brandon was the one who sent me in here. Girl, he's got it bad for you. Thank God he's no longer with LaTasha. Ugh, I can't stand that girl. You are a much better choice."

Jazz looked up at Lyric, pleased and surprised. And thankful. Lyric was a straight shooter. If she thought Jazz was worthy of Brandon, then maybe that little voice was wrong.

"Thank you for saying that, Lyric," she said, her voice catching in her throat.

"It's true," Lyric said, shrugging her shoulders. She caught Jazz's eye in the mirror and smiled. "Take your time. I'll stall Mr. Hotness for you. But don't be too long, in here or you know, with him, 'cause the boy is fire, as you know."

Jazz managed a small laugh, "Alright, I'll be right out."

"Cool."

Lyric reached for the door.

"Hey, Lyric?"

The girl paused and looked back at Jazz, her hand still gripping the door handle as she raised her eyebrows in response.

"Really, though, thank you."

Lyric pulled the door open. "No worries." She took a step before letting the door shut again. "I don't want to weird you out again, but I was, um, wondering...."

Jazz looked at her, waiting.

"Well, I mean, Landi gave just about everyone a nickname, but all she ever called me was Lyric."

Jazz smiled, finally something she could answer both easily and truthfully. "She called you Lyric because she liked you."

A look of confusion passed across the girl's face. She looked back at Jazz doubtfully.

"If you remember," Jazz replied softly. "All she ever called me was Jazz."

CHAPTER NINETEEN
TEMPTATION IS CLOSE AT HAND

By the time the day ended, Jazz was mentally exhausted. Again. She'd been called out of her sixth period class to talk with the school mental health counselor. She had performed a difficult balancing act of trying to appear as if she was healing while admitting she was still hurting. Jazz hoped she'd come up with the right mix to satisfy whatever mental balance the counselor was looking for.

After school, she hurried to her locker and rushed out to her car, trying to avoid getting caught up in any conversations with her so-called friends. She'd almost made it to her car when she heard her name being called out. She turned to see Brandon jogging after her, looking cool, athletic, and hot all at once.

Jazz looked up at the sky, "Why God, why?"

"Man, you can move pretty quick for a cheerleader," he said as he jogged even with her, easily matching her pace.

"I don't even know what that means," Jazz answered, slowing down to a more normal pace. "Don't be a sexist pig."

"Well, you know, it's not like you're a jock or anything."

"I'll have you know that cheerleading is a sport. We cheerleaders are athletes."

"You think so, do you?"

"Well, I'd like to see you and your boys on the b-ball squad try to perform synchronized backflips into splits."

"Do we have to wear cute little skirts while we do it?"

Jazz glared at him as they stopped at her car, a million witty retorts flying through her head. She wasn't in the mood.

"Okay, well, see ya tomorrow," Jazz said in the friendliest tone she could muster while still implying that he could go.

"Whoa, slow your roll, there shorty, you still owe me a date."

"I'm not short," retorted Jazz, ignoring the part of his sentence that sent electricity dancing up and down her spine.

Brandon burst out laughing. He rested a heavy forearm on the top of her head, "Well, from waaayyy up here, you look pretty short."

"I'll have you know that I'm 5'4", which is average height for a woman, now if I was, say 5'3" or something, then you could have called me short accurately, however, since I'm taller than that, I am not, in fact, short, but average."

Brandon laughed again, "What you are is adorable."

Jazz had no retort for that, which caused Brandon to smirk happily.

"I have finally found a way to quiet the great and powerful Jazz Sanders," Brandon said, chuckling. "Who knew? A simple but true compliment renders her speechless. Cool, let's try another one. I also think you are very brave."

Jazz opened her mouth but couldn't think of something to say. Brandon hooted with laughter again before taking a step closer to Jazz, which caused her to immediately think that it would be a good time to examine her shoes. She dropped her head and gazed intently at her ballet flats. Brandon cupped her chin gently and raised her face. While his smile was gone, his eyes were gentle. Jazz's heart skipped a beat.

"I know how much you are hurting," he said softly. "And I can see the effort it takes for you to pretend not to be upset all the time. It's cool that you are putting on such a brave face for everyone else, but you can be real with me. I think I've already told you that, though, right?"

Jazz looked up at him for a moment before furrowing her brow and frowning at him. "Who are you? I mean, don't you know you're a 17-year-old boy? Aren't you supposed to be trying to capitalize on my grief and coax me into situations where you can benefit from my poor judgment? You do realize you have a reputation for being a dog, right? I mean, honestly, you aren't normal! You're like some character out of some romance novel set in the times of dukes and lords and crap! What is with you?"

Brandon grinned, "Hello, I'm being raised by not one but two psychologists! I'm very sensitive and insightful, much like Essay. But, uh, don't get it twisted. If there is some way I can get you into a compromising situation and take advantage, I will definitely do that. I may be sensitive, but I ain't crazy. You are seriously cute, you know. And your body is smoking. Short, but smoking. I'll definitely hit that if I get a chance."

"Ha! You aren't going to silence me with the mere word cute! Or smokin' either! And all that other stuff is seriously sexist. You can't say stuff like that anymore!" yelped Jazz, ignoring the note of hysterical shrillness that crept into her voice. "I gotta go! And just so you know, it's not because I'm afraid of you and your compliments. I'm very busy! Like a bee. Bzzz."

The sparks flying between them and all this yummy tension felt like it was leading to something wonderful that she didn't deserve. It was time to bail, and quickly.

"Now where are you running off to?" Brandon asked, leaning on the driver's side door and blocking her from the handle. "You need to explain why you think I'm a dog. You can't just drop that bomb then flee."

He crossed his arms and gave her a lopsided grin and waited.

It was all Jazz could do to stop herself from stamping her foot in frustration. No one their age should be so tempting. It was unreal.

"You know why, look at your snap story," she said pointedly, waving him away from her car door. "This is harassment. I'm sure your parents would both agree. Move. Please. I gotta go."

"Are you going someplace I can go?" he said sweetly. He looked into her eyes, reached over, and started playing with one of her braids. Jazz felt her knees buckle slightly.

Warning bells sounded in her head. Jazz intended on heading home, wanting desperately to curl up in bed and pretend that the world didn't exist. Saying she was going to go home would not be enough to dissuade him. She needed to come up with a destination that would turn him off. An escape plan formulated in her head as she swatted his hand away.

"To the Children's Hospital," she blurted out, picking the one place that had not only been on her mind but that would guarantee that he would leave her alone.

"Cool, I finished my application over the weekend. I'll go with you. I just happen to have it here in my backpack."

"What! Application? What's going on? Why do you have an application?" Jazz squeaked at him, the hysterical tone back.

Brandon's lips curled into a lazy smile. He looked somewhat like a cat who'd just cornered a fat, juicy mouse.

"Your girl, Landi, gave me an intern packet like five or six weeks ago. She said you would be volunteering there soon and that the Sibling Sanctuary needed male volunteers. She was going on about how you and I would be a good pair of interns for it. I think she was trying to play matchmaker, but even if you weren't going to work there, I'd have volunteered anyway once she told me about it. She must have overheard me talking about being a counselor at a kid's basketball camp last summer and thought I'd be interested. Plus, it will look crazy good on the college apps. Shit, knowing Landi, though, it was probably a mixture of both. She could be a bossy busy body sometimes. Plus, to be honest, I don't think she liked me very much, but that didn't stop her from trying to get me to volunteer. She was kinda always up in everyone's business like that."

Jazz frowned at him. Even if he was a stupid hot, tall, delicious, brown-skinned hottie who was ridiculously kind and stuff, he shouldn't be speaking about her best friend like that.

Even if he was right.

For a moment, both of them stood silently. She let her eyes drift over his shoulders; between the soft look of concern in his eyes and the words about her best friend, it was an effort to keep from tearing up.

"Well, let's go," he said, breaking the silence with a cheerful tone. "You drive. Your car probably still smells new, while mine just smells. You know that vape smell lingers. I've told my boys to not do it in my car, but you know how they act sometimes. No home-training. I don't know why they think it don't smell. I mean, it's not as disgusting as actual cigarettes, but it def has a scent. Don't know how anyone who calls themselves an athlete would do that mess, but whatever. To each their own."

Jazz brought his face back into focus and scowled at him.

Brandon grinned, stepped to the side, and tried to open the door for her.

"Come on, cutie pie, unlock the door and allow me," he said, adding an exaggerated bow.

Jazz glared up at him some more before heaving a sigh and unlocking her door. He opened the door and bowed again, this time while doffing his baseball cap. Jazz growled audibly at him.

Jazz left Brandon and his application at the front desk and checked into the SibSanc. Moments later, Brandon appeared into what Jazz had thought of as her sanctuary, escorted by Grandma Daisy. He gave her a jaunty wave, as did Grandma Daisy, before turning to enter the glassed-in art/eating area and began talking animatedly. She couldn't help but glance over every few seconds to see how his induction process was going. There was a confusing mix of emotions bouncing around her brain, and she didn't know which one she should focus on. There was a feeling of annoyance at Brandon; how dare he try to ruin her grief and penitence by overpowering those emotions with her ever-deepening attraction for him. How would she ever be able to feel properly sad about Landi if the joy she felt about him being so clearly interested in going out with her kept interfering? This must be some sort of test from God, or perhaps a temptation sent by Satan.

Then there was the fact that having him volunteer sounded like too much fun. No matter how hard Jazz racked her brain, she couldn't figure out how having fun with Brandon, even while volunteering, would achieve any of the acts of penance she'd googled. She could, however, think that not being with him would come closer to fulfilling one of the items than anything else.

Try as she might, she couldn't figure out how Brandon related to any of the required acts of penance. Feeding and clothing the poor? Nope. There was the visiting sick people requirement, and Jazz was counting on the fact that even if the kids in the SibSanc weren't sick, she was in a hospital, near sick people, so maybe she'd get some points. She'd given away some clothes last week, which left food, ransom money, and burying the dead. Maybe she'd just kill Brandon and then bury him. Of course, killing him would almost definitely negate all the other acts of charity and mercy she'd done lately, and then she'd be right back at square one.

Ransoming the captive? She still didn't get what that meant.

Despite her best efforts, it seemed that God was going to make forgiveness for Landi dying all but unattainable. She chanced another glance at Brandon. He caught her eye and winked. Her stomach did a back somersault, and she felt her mouth form into a smile. Luckily, she caught herself before it got too big, and she stuck her tongue out at him instead. He grinned at her before turning his attention back to Grandma Daisy, who appeared to be asking him something about his application. Jazz didn't know what she wanted more at that moment: to kill him or kiss him.

A few moments later, while Jazz was getting ready to start a movie for a little boy, Miss Ruth scurried in, looking as surly and cross as ever. Jazz bit back a groan before realizing that Miss Ruth, and her cranky demeanor, made the whole place less pleasant. Which was a good thing, right? After all, serving penance shouldn't be fun, and Miss Ruth's mere presence sucked a bunch of joy right out of the place.

"What are you doing here?" she snapped at Jazz.

"Helping?"

"Hmph," grunted Miss Ruth before jerking a thumb towards the art center. "It's Monday, not Friday. Who's that talking with Daisy?"

"Brandon, a guy from my school, he's going to volunteer here too. They're going over his application."

"He your boyfriend?"

"Mine? No, not really, I mean, no. I can't, he's only my, not mine, my, I mean, he, Brandon, Brandon's only a friend. We aren't going out. Cause I shouldn't... I mean. No, he's not my boyfriend."

Jazz felt her cheeks grow warm under the beady-eyed scrutiny Miss Ruth was giving her. Jazz shrugged and glanced over at the art center. Brandon chose that moment to look dead into her eyes and give her a smile — a toe-curling, body-warming smile. She automatically grinned back. Beside her, Jazz heard Miss Ruth snort derisively.

"You said you aren't going out?"

"Well, no," muttered Jazz, not meeting the older woman's eye. "We aren't."

"He come here with you?"

"Well, yes, but...."

"He come here because of you?"

"Um, no?" Jazz paused, hearing the questioning tone in her voice. "I mean, no. No. Landi got him to fill out the application," she repeated with a more certain air.

"Hmph." Miss Ruth stood there, hands on her hips, and looking fixedly at Jazz before asking, "Was he Landi's boyfriend?"

"Oh, no! She likes..." Jazz said quickly before stopping herself mid-sentence.

Miss Ruth raised a gray eyebrow at her.

"Landi liked someone else," finished Jazz, swallowing the ever-present knot in her throat.

Miss Ruth looked over at Brandon, then back at Jazz before uttering another grunt. For a moment, they stood together, Jazz trying not to glance over at Brandon, feeling the heat of Miss Ruth's stare. Fortunately, the little boy waiting for a movie called over to Jazz, who felt immense relief at being able to escape the company of the old sourpuss as she hustled over to help him.

As she made a big production out of settling the little boy in the movie nook, Brandon and Grandma Daisy emerged from their meeting. Jazz watched surreptitiously as Grandma Daisy introduced him to Miss Ruth and then stared after them in confusion as they both left the SibSanc. Although curious about what exactly was going on with Brandon, Jazz was happy to have him away from her for a while, so she could focus on why she was there in the first place.

As more kids trickled in, Jazz clicked into a groove, welcoming the newcomers, giving tours to the first-timers, doling out hugs to the few regulars she knew, and providing snacks and comfort as necessary. After a while, there came a lull in the action, giving her a chance to relax for a few minutes. As she was settling into the cushy chair in the castle, she saw Miss Ruth stalking over to her, and she groaned inwardly. Jazz popped up and headed towards the tea party room, under the pretense of straightening up the area. Miss Ruth veered in her direction, and Jazz looked around for an escape route, but she was trapped.

"You didn't say that your friend," Miss Ruth smirked and used her fingers to indicate quotation marks around the word friend, causing Jazz to clench her teeth, "Was Dr. McGee's son."

"I, well," stuttered Jazz, trying to keep her growing irritation with the woman from coloring her tone of voice. "You didn't ask."

"Well, he is."

"Yes, I know. Both of his parents are doctors, psychologists, actually."

"How nice for him," snipped Miss Ruth. "At any rate, I'm sure his helping," those two fingers reappeared, "here is just a formality. Something for his college application. Daisy took him down to get his pass—in case you wanted to know where your 'friend' disappeared to." Her fingers wagging again.

Jazz resisted the urge to use a very specific one of her fingers in response to the woman's sarcasm. Instead, through gritted teeth, she replied, "Oh, okay, thanks," as politely as she could manage. Jazz then tried to step politely away from Miss Ruth. Unfortunately, the woman wasn't finished yet. She took a closing step toward Jazz.

"His mother's got admittance privileges here as well. As far as I know, she too is a respected psychologist around here."

Jazz nodded, having nothing to add to that little tidbit of information.

"Oh, and in case you were wondering, he introduced himself as your boyfriend."

Jazz's mouth dropped open.

"Shut up!"

"I beg your pardon?"

"Sorry! Excuse me, it's only a saying. I mean, he didn't, did he?"

"I just said that he did."

"Yes, but did he really?"

Miss Ruth rolled her eyes in annoyance.

Jazz sank into a miniature chair, muttering to herself, "This is no good. Oh, geez. This is a hot mess."

"He seems like a nice young man, said Miss Ruth. "Most boys his age are too busy being thuggish and shopping for pants that don't fit properly on their backsides to want to do anything like this. Even for a cute girl. Plus, he spoke right up and used proper English."

"I know," moaned Jazz. "He's a freak like that."

"He does not appear to be a freak at all," Miss Ruth said with much more irritation than Jazz thought necessary. "He appeared to be a nice young man. I'd hold on to him if I were you."

"I know he's not a freak freak. He's a not like most guys my age type of freak. And I can't hold on to him. I mean, I'd like to, I mean, who wouldn't? But it's not right. He's not mine to hold, anyway."

Why she was telling any of this to an imposing, old busybody was beyond her. Jazz closed her mouth and made a big show of cleaning up, hoping that Miss Ruth would catch the hint.

She didn't.

"Are you going out with someone else?" asked Miss Ruth. Jazz bit back a sigh before looking up at her.

"Well, no, but...."

"Is he going out with someone else?"

"No, ma'am, it's not that...."

"Then what's the problem? Surely it can't be his looks. He's a nice-looking boy. I mean, he could use a haircut. Why these boys today like all that mess on the top of their heads is beyond me. However, he seems intelligent enough for a teenager. He clearly likes you, based on the mooning looks he was sending your way. Not to mention the fact that he proclaimed himself your suitor. And, it's also readily apparent that you are smitten with him, based on the stuttering and stammering you are doing right now. You can barely put together a full sentence, for goodness sake."

Miss Ruth crossed her arms and looked down at Jazz, waiting for a reply.

"It's not that simple. I don't think I should... You see, I...." Jazz closed her mouth and put a hand to her forehead. Her eyes filled with tears. God, was she tired of crying. The thoughts rattling around in her head were too painful to say out loud. She didn't deserve someone like Brandon. She wasn't due any happiness, certainly not now, so soon after the accident, and maybe not ever. She hadn't done nearly enough to earn forgiveness for what she'd done to Landi. And until she was sure that God didn't hate her, she wouldn't feel right about being with Brandon or anyone. She wasn't worthy of joy. But that wasn't any business of Miss Ruth's, so rather than spill her guts, Jazz pulled on a fake smile, "Brandon's a kidder. He was joking around. Besides, I'm sure I'm not the only girl around that he calls a girlfriend. I'll get him later for it, don't worry."

Miss Ruth didn't return her smile. Instead, she looked steadily at Jazz as if she were analyzing her, then without another word, she turned around and headed back to the check-in desk, leaving Jazz standing alone in the tea party area, filled with joy at Brandon's words, and with sorrow as well.

CHAPTER TWENTY
THE SUN KEEPS RISING

It was the doorbell that woke Jazz up on a bright Saturday morning in the middle of May, out of one of the soundest nights of sleep she'd had in weeks. In the distance, she heard familiar voices talking with her parents. Barely a minute later, there was a knock on her bedroom door.

"Jazz?"

Jazz sat up in her bed as her mother came into her room, looking anxious. "Jazz, you need to get up and get dressed, please. Quickly. Then come down to the living room."

Her mother left, and Jazz listened as her footsteps hurried down the stairs.

Minutes later, Jazz had showered and dressed. It was only 9:30 in the morning, but she heard what sounded like a roomful of people as she slowly came down the stairs. As she walked in, the noise abruptly stopped. There was indeed a crowd of people in her living room. She came to a sudden halt at the doorway. Out of force of habit, she raised her hand in greeting and whispered a "Hello" that no one could have possibly heard. She received weak waves back from Mr. and Mrs. Lewis, who sat on the couch clutching each other's hands. From Linny and his brother Malachi, who stood in a far corner of the room with their arms crossed, she received only sullen, blatantly unfriendly stares. Landi's remaining brothers, Micah, Lamont, and Maddox, stood behind their parents. They gave her half-hearted, confused waves as well as if they didn't know whether it was allowed to greet her with their usual friendliness or not. Like hip hop bodyguards, her parents bustled over to her. They stood on either side of her as if protecting her from overzealous fans. They bundled her over to the loveseat where the three of them sat jammed together, her mother clutching her hand and kneading it like bread while her father kept patting her on the knee.

The silence of so many usually loud and chatty people lay heavily upon the room, like a thick musty blanket. No one seemed to have anything to say: a historic first amongst both the Sanders and the Lewises. The tension of the situation instantly made Jazz's stomach queasy. She swallowed the bile rising in her throat, embarrassingly aware that her gulps were the only sounds in the room.

Jazz felt her mother tighten her grip on her hand to an almost painful level. Her father suddenly cleared his throat as if he were about to speak, the sound making Mrs. Lewis jump. Heads swiveled in his direction. He gave a slight smile and a little shrug but said nothing. After a few minutes of sitting in this uncomfortable room,

Jazz wondered why the Lewis' were here and what they all could be waiting for together. Another five minutes passed as Jazz sat quietly, avoiding looking at the other side of the room, her knee being patted every few seconds, and her hand being kneaded, and then the doorbell rang. Her mother pried herself from out of the loveseat and walked swiftly off to open the door. She returned quickly, followed by a uniformed police officer who came into the living room and pulled off his hat.

Jazz's heart leaped in her chest like a frog hopped up on caffeine, feeling as though it was trying to burst out of her chest. Her stomach roiled violently, and her mouth went dry all at once. Her blood pressure shot up so much that her head started to throb, the beginnings of a stress headache began pounding behind her right eye. She began hearing a weird buzzing in her ears as her heartbeat quickened. She let her eyes slide out of focus and concentrated on breathing.

In and out, in and out, she chanted in her head. In and out, in and out.

When she felt calmer, she refocused her eyes on her tennis shoes, staring at the very tips, wondering vaguely when that grass streak had appeared on them.

"Good morning, folks. I'm Officer Pettis, from District Five." Jazz heard the people mutter quiet greetings, and with tremendous effort Jazz raised her eyes to the officer and gave him a curt nod before lowering her eyes quickly, staring down at her hands and wondering vaguely why they weren't blue.

Officer Pettis nodded and continued, "Thanks so much for agreeing to all meet here," the officer said, addressing the room. "Situations like these are rare when both parties can actually agree to meet somewhere outside of the precinct, together." He glanced around the room.

Mrs. Lewis spoke quietly from her seat. "We are all family, Officer. We will hear what you have to say together."

If this statement surprised Officer Pettis, he hid it well, saying with a shrug, "Don't think we have a room at the station that could have fit all of you all. And it's nice not to have to say all this twice. So, folks, I've got the final incident report here, and it's pretty brief, so I won't be taking up too much of your time this Saturday morning."

Jazz heard him from somewhere deep inside of herself. She couldn't stop thinking about her fingers. How they felt frozen and stiff as if all the blood had been drained from them and her veins filled with ice water instead. Her fingers were as cold and unmoving as ice blocks. Popsicle fingers attached to the ends of her hands. Jazz had the absurd thought that if she tried, she could snap her fingers off her hands like icicles from a roof. She wiggled them a little and watched them move, feeling amazed to see them functioning properly.

"Okay, let's see," said Officer Pettis, adopting an official, neutral, yet commanding tone. "On Friday, March 28th, of this year, at approximately 11:40 p.m., Jazz Lynn Sanders, age 16 - and 6-months driver of 2006 Honda Civic, ran into two bull elk on Route 47. Killed in the resulting crash was passenger Landi Renee Lewis, age 17 and 3 months, the only passenger. Cause of death, blunt force trauma to neck and spine. It was determined that the victim did not have her seat belt on at the time of the crash, causing her to be projected through the windshield resulting in her fatal injuries."

"Final toxicology reports show that the driver, Miss Sanders, had 0% alcohol in her blood system. Likewise, the passenger, Miss Lewis, had no trace of alcohol in her blood system. No trace of any narcotic, no THC, methamphetamine, or any other illegal substance was found in Miss Lewis' blood system, nor was any found in Miss Sander's blood system. The length of the skid marks from the crash indicates that the driver was traveling between 34 and 39 miles per hour. Posted speed limit of that section of Route 47 is 35 miles per hour."

Here the Officer paused. Jazz glanced up at him and saw that he was turning to address her parents more directly.

"In summary, Mr. and Mrs. Sanders, your daughter, was driving within the time frame of the county's legal curfew, close to or at the posted legal speed limit, and was not under the influence of either alcohol or drugs of any kind."

Jazz heard her mother breathe an audible sigh of relief, followed by a squeeze to her hand that hurt. Her father patted her on the knee, and Jazz could feel some of the tension leave his body.

Officer Pettis flipped through his papers and paused again. Jazz saw him take a deep breath as if unhappy about what he was going to have to say next. He turned and faced the Lewis side of the room. "As I've mentioned, Ms. Lewis did not have her seat belt on at the time of impact. Based on the investigator's opinion, this was the sole reason she died. In terms of the cause of the crash, as I'm sure you know, having lived in the area, during this time of year, herds of elk are often seen foraging for food in that area. There are posted signs to watch for deer, although none within half a mile of the crash site. Based on reports from the Department of Wildlife, a rather large herd of elk have been seen roaming in the vicinity of the crash frequently during the past month."

Jazz heard sobs coming from the other side of the room. Inside her shoes, she clenched and unclenched her toes, trying to ignore the urge she felt to cry.

Squeeze release, squeeze, release.

Strong, firm toes, that's what all the girls need! Jazz stifled an insane urge to giggle.

It'd always irritated Landi how Jazz used humor in the darkest of moments. That thought sobered her up quickly.

Officer Pettis had paused for a moment, allowing his news to sink in. He pulled out a sheet. The room was silent as everyone waited for what was coming next.

"Okay, so, generally speaking, bull elks weight close to 700 lbs. Based on the DofW report, the bull elk that was hit and killed in the crash last Friday weighed a whopping 755 lbs. Based on the damage to the car, it appears that another elk was at least grazed by the car, if not hit as solidly as the first." Officer Pettis stopped talking, and Jazz looked up to see that he was looking at her for confirmation. She nodded brusquely and looked back down at her hands. He continued, "It is very fortunate that no other fatalities occurred."

Intellectually, Jazz knew that what the Officer was saying was true and factual. She also supposed that it should, in some way, make her feel better. In fact, the way he was saying it made it look as if she wasn't at all at fault. One, she hadn't been drunk. Or, two, high. Three, she hadn't been speeding, or four, out past curfew. All of this was true and factual, and to hear this said so officially by someone who was unbiased should have meant something to her. These facts should exonerate her.

And, based on the look on the Officer's face, as well as the expressions on Mr. and Mrs. Lewis's faces, Jazz should be feeling comforted, vindicated, even. But she didn't. Not a little bit. Even though she could feel the bodies of her parents, who'd been sitting so stiffly and rigidly on either side of her, relax, the report still meant nothing to her. Even the fact that when she dared to chance a glance across the room, she saw that Mrs. Lewis was casting an "I told you so look" over at her two sons, Linny and Malachi meant nothing. None of this did anything to relieve any of the suffocating guilt that was now a part of her.

Jazz felt no feeling of relief. Grief and sadness still lay upon her, coloring everything gray. Sorrow's clammy arms were still wrapped deeply around her, keeping her a prisoner within them. This report would give her no sense of forgiveness or acquittal. No impressions that she was free to go on with her life. Of this, she was dead certain. Instead, Jazz knew, without a doubt, that she was simply an observer in this "official report." For all it meant to her, she could have easily been sitting watching a dry documentary on television about a crash she'd heard about but hadn't been in.

This report that Officer Pettis was giving, in her expert opinion, was not an accurate recounting of the event, which was the worst moment of her life. No, this "final," "official" investigative report was a dry and lifeless list of interesting facts. And while Jazz knew that these details described what had happened that night, at least for the others, she didn't feel as if the report painted a true picture of the actual event.

For instance, this "official" report didn't mention that Jazz could still remember the fleeting feeling of cold metal against the side of her hand as she accidentally knocked her phone from Landi's hand. It didn't report the dull thump her phone made when it landed somewhere in the back seat. Nor did it say anything about the muddled ringtone that sounded indicating that another text had come in, or the metallic click of the seat belt as Landi unbuckled it so she could reach the phone, or the happy sound of Landi's screaming laughter as she leaned over her seat trying to get the errant phone.

No.

This report was full of weights, and speeds, and percentages. It told nothing.

Sounds. And sights. And feelings.

The stupid report was missing the sounds and the sights of that night. Officer Pettis hadn't read a description of how hard they both were laughing seconds before Jazz turned back to face the road and saw the elk in the middle of the street. Or how her body felt when the sudden flood of adrenaline coursed through her body as she slammed on the brake. Or how it felt like she was putting her foot through the floor of her car, or how she could still hear the high-pitched squealing of her tires as her car skidded relentlessly toward the elk. What about how the elks' eyes glowed eerily in her headlights as they stood stock-still instead of getting out of her damn way like any smart animal should have?

Nor did the Officer say anything about the double thud and crunch as the car hit first one, then the other elk, or the explosive yet strangely pretty tinkling sound the windshield made as it shattered when Landi sailed through it.

If the investigator who wrote this so-called "complete" report had been thorough, they would have described how being hit by the airbag felt like a punch in the stomach and face at the same time. It would have told everyone about how loud the whooshing gasp she made was as her breath was forced from her body from its impact. Officer Pettis should have told everyone about the eerie moaning sound the dying bull elk made and how it convulsed and twitched as it died in the road. Or about the uneven clip-clop sound the hooves of the other injured elk made as it limped away from the scene and back into the woods.

Sound wasn't the only thing missing either. That night had its share of smells, too, none of which Officer Pettis mentioned as he read. What about the acrid, slightly metallic smell of the powder from the airbag? Or how it mingled with the musty, wet dog-like smell of the bull elk? And the sounds and smells are absolutely nothing compared to the sights from that night. The most glaring lack of important information was how silent and unmoving Landi was as she lay in the street. Or how Jazz sat motionless in the car, listening to it click, ting, and bing, wishing with all her might that Landi would sit up? Just move her head or wiggle her feet or make any movement at all, even a little one. Surely that should be part of a "complete" and "final" report.

Was he going to tell everyone about how Jazz still didn't even know who called 911? Or how long she sat gasping in the car watching Landi lay in the road through her rearview mirror? Or how confused she was at first to be facing the wrong direction on the road? Did he know how much time passed before there was an unknown woman telling her that help was on the way and that she should try to breathe deeply and slowly? What about how all she could do was nod her head and stare at Landi's motionless body?

If he was here to tell what happened, then, as far as Jazz was concerned, the report he read was woefully and pitifully free of any real information.

Jazz raised her eyes to stare at Officer Pettis, who was flipping through his papers, feeling angry and annoyed at his lack of accurate detail. On her right, she could feel her mother's grip on her hand slacken and relax, while on her left, her father's nervous knee patting ceased. She chanced a longer glance across the room and saw that both Mrs. and Mrs. Lewis looked relieved, unbelievably sad, but relieved, as did Micah, Lamont, and Maddox. She quickly looked away from that group before they saw her and thought to smile reassuringly at her. She couldn't have born that undeserved forgiving gesture. Instead,

Jazz looked over at Linny and Malachi, whose faces had morphed from angry to numb. While she had to admit that numb was better than what she'd gotten earlier, it was still not great. Not that she deserved great, but still...

Jazz returned her gaze to the center of the room where, by the grim set of Officer Pettis' lips as he finally settled on a page, Jazz knew his report was not over.

"Okay, so, recovered at the scene, among the personal effects of both girls, a cell phone belonging to Jazz. And a cell phone belonging to Landi. The tech analysis department report shows cell phone activity at the time of the crash, on the driver's phone."

The atmosphere of the room suddenly shifted.

"I knew it!" Jazz heard Linny hiss from across the room. It felt like a slap. Her mother's limp hand re-tightened into a death grip, and seconds later the tips of Jazz's hands tingled. Her father replaced his hand on her leg, squeezing tightly, as if in warning rather than the reassuring patting from earlier.

Officer Pettis shot a quelling look in Linny's direction before continuing, "There were text messages which started at 11:34. They've been transcribed as follows: From number 373-609-0510 the number belonging to an unknown person and 729-209-1190 the cell number belonging to Jazz Lynn Sanders."

"What time did you say the accident took place, Officer?" interrupted Malachi, his deep voice reverberating around the room.

Officer Pettis flipped back a couple pages, scanning the report before answering, "Approximately 11:40 p.m."

"And the texting begins when?" Linny asked through clenched teeth.

"11:34."

Through her pants, she could feel her father's nails bite into her thigh, and her mother sucked in a breath and squeezed so tightly on Jazz's hand that her fingers folded over one another.

"Hmph!" snorted Linny. "Knew it."

"Linwood!" chastised his mother. "I'm sorry, Officer, please continue."

"The transcript of the texts is as follows:

From number 373-609-0510 received at 11:34 p.m.: Yo Jazz

"Um, to make this go a bit faster, I'll just use the names as it appears in the contacts if you don't mind."

The room gave a murmur of agreement.

"Thanks, the exchange is between Jazz's phone and someone recorded in the contacts as Fine Ass Brandon."

Jazz fervently wished for the loveseat to swallow her up.

"I'll shorten it to Brandon if you don't mind." There was a moment of silence, and Jazz looked up to see that the officer was waiting for agreement. She nodded miserably.

"Jazz sent at 11:34: I'm sorry Jazz is driving, as you well know. She can't come to her phone right now. This is the badass Landi texting. What do you want?"

The officer stopped reading. "So, um, clearly, this is your daughter Landi texting, so while I'll say Jazz since it is her number, please note that it is Landi texting until I note otherwise."

Jazz assumed everyone nodded at the Officer because he continued reading. As he read, she could picture the text chain in her head.

Brandon received at 11:35: `I want Jazz Tell your girl She's smokin' hot and I'm all about her`

Jazz sent at 11:35: `Wow So romantic Whatev So what did your boy Ty say about me?`

Brandon received at 11:35: `We ain't females. We don't talk like that`

Jazz sent at 11:35: `Bullshit. I have 2 many brothers to believe that Ya'll are worse than we r`

Brandon received at 11:35: `Whatev Tell Jazz 2 call me when she gets home`

Jazz sent at 11:36: `Not until you tell me what Tyrone said about me`

Jazz sent 11:36: `I know he was digging me Just tell me Or I'll tell Jazz this text is her mom And delete all this`

Brandon received 11:37: `Damn Lan He ain't even by me right now`

Jazz sent 11:38 `I think my girl Jazz is too good for you anyway`

Brandon received at 11:38: `I'm serious tho I like her for real Tell her Imma facetime her later tonight`

Brandon received 11:38: Landi just give Jazz her phone back But do me a solid and delete this cause I sound mad corny

Brandon received 11:39: Yo you know what I don't even care In fact show her right now

Jazz sent 11:38: Damn you stupid she's driving!!!!!!! I won't even show her the screen Besides, you ain't even answered my question about Ty

Brandon received 11:38: tell her I think she's the next Mrs. Brandon McGee

Jazz sent 11:38: So are you drunk or just full of yourself? You ain't all that I may tell her if you tell ME what your boy says about me

Brandon received 11:39: show her You're not the boss of me Besides the future Mrs. McGee can read all this when she gets home anyway

Jazz sent 11:39: fool please Not if I delete it I ain't showing

Officer Pettis paused for a moment, looking a bit embarrassed. "Um, there's a little picture, er, emoji, of, um, dog poo after that sentence."

If Jazz hadn't felt so mortified by this, she would have laughed. Instead, she felt embarrassed and bare. As if they'd all seen her coming out of the shower naked. After clearing his throat, Officer Pettis continued.

Brandon received 11:39: why you so mean Landi? Dang

Jazz sent 11:39: Mean? Don't get it twisted
Imma delete all these messages It's easy
Don't tempt me.

Brandon received 11:39: Jesus hold on Imma go
find him

Jazz sent 11:39: I'll wait

Jazz sent 11:39: Be quick about it

Brandon received 11:41: I can't find him.

Brandon received 11:41: Landi I'm serious I
can't find that fool

Brandon 11:41: I'm telling the truth Landi
But Imma hook you up when we leave

Brandon received 11:43: Landi just give Jazz
back her phone

Brandon received 11:45: Jazz you home yet?

Brandon received 11:46: Landi ya'll home?

Brandon received 12:01: Yo Jazz You up?

Officer Pettis stopped reading, and the room was silent save for the ticking of the grandfather clock over the fireplace mantle.

"So there's more of the young man texting after that, but I won't read it as it's not germane to the investigation."

Jazz sat there feeling as if her body temperature had raised a thousand degrees. She figured it was from the nauseating mix of emotions coursing through her body. It was equal parts horror, embarrassment, and mortification. That's what she was feeling. Horrorembarrassfication. It may not be a real word, but it should have been. Jazz concentrated on the grass streak on her shoe, refusing to look up. While nothing could come close to being as horrible as the night of the accident. This moment certainly was coming in a close second.

After a minute, the officer cleared his throat before saying, "So clearly, based on the transcript which we believe is fairly accurate, we had to translate some of their text speak shortcuts into proper English for the report, but we are fairly certain that the texted conversation seems to have taken place between the owner of the phone 323-609-0510, a Brandon Elmer McGee, and Miss Lewis, on Ms. Sanders' cell phone. We are certain that this is the case because of the content of the conversation. Meaning, that Jazz was not texting and driving."

The room was silent, and despite how heavy her heartfelt, Jazz had to suppress a manic giggle at hearing Brandon's middle name was Elmer. In her head, she heard the echo of Landi giving an exasperated sigh. She squeezed her hands into fists, digging her nails into the flesh of her palms.

The officer reached into the manila envelope he was holding and pulled out two cell phones, Landi's gold I-phone, and Jazz's Droid. He handed Landi's phone to her mother, who immediately burst into tears. After patting Mrs. Lewis awkwardly on the shoulder, he turned and handed Jazz her phone, which now sported a cracked screen. Well, a worse cracked screen.

"Um, we charged your phone to retrieve the messages for the purposes of the investigation. Since then, it has been ringing and binging quite a bit. That first Saturday, we were forced to stick it in a drawer. The ringing and buzzing were driving us crazy. None of us could figure out how to put it on silent." The officer let out a lame little chuckle at his joke. When no one else in the room laughed, he cleared his throat and returned to his official police demeanor.

"Anyway, finally, we let it die. So, it needs charging, but aside from the cracked screen appears to be working fine."

Jazz nodded and took the phone, not wanting to touch it. She placed it on the coffee table in front of her and stared at it like it was a giant cockroach. She would not have been at all surprised to see it scuttle off the table and under the couch.

Officer Pettis returned to his place in the middle of the room again and began flipping through the report once more. He cleared his throat again. Much to Jazz's annoyance, it was clearly a nervous tic he had.

"So, that's it. Are there any questions?"

Jazz felt her mother flinch a bit and looked up.

Mrs. Lewis had composed herself and had her hand raised in the air as if she were a second grader in math class.

"So that we are clear, Jazz is not at fault, and there will be no charges against her?"

Jazz felt her insides freeze. Her mother threw a protective arm around her and glared at the officer.

"No, ma'am. Jazz was the victim of poor timing and a larger than usual herd of roaming elk. Honestly, it could have happened to anyone on that road that night."

"Good," Mrs. Lewis said in almost a shout. "She's a wonderful girl. I know this has been as hard on her as it has been on us. I'd hate for her life to be impacted negatively because of this."

Jazz looked over at Mrs. Lewis through tear-filled eyes and saw Mr. Lewis nod in agreement before throwing his arm around his wife and pulling her closer to him. An intense wave of guilt washed over Jazz. They didn't know the whole story. She should tell them. She should open her mouth right this instant and say that Landi only took off her seatbelt because Jazz had knocked the phone out of her hand. She should confess that the only reason they were even out at the Wash was because Jazz had insisted they go so she could chase after Brandon. She should admit to them all that despite what Officer Pettis just said, it was indeed her fault. She was the reason that Landi was lying in Forest Lawn Cemetery rather than sitting at their kitchen table eating a big stack of her father's blueberry pancakes and getting ready to go get a pedicure and manicure with her mother.

Silence still filled the room, and Jazz felt her parents jump when Officer Pettis cleared his throat for the umpteenth time and said, "Could I bother you folks for some water?"

As if pricked by a pin, Jazz leaped out of her seat, "I'll get it, sir." She hurried out of the living room and into the kitchen, happy for a reason to be out of that room. She stood for a second, looking around the kitchen, feeling as if she hadn't been in the room for decades. Jazz grabbed a glass out of the cabinet and filled it to the brim with ice and water, letting out a shuddering sigh. She watched her hand in amazement as the glass shook so violently that she spilled some water onto the floor.

Out. That's what she needed to be. Out of this room, out of this house, out. So rather than carrying the glass of water into the next room for the officer, Jazz sat the glass on the counter, grabbed her purse off the kitchen table, opened the back door, got into her car, and drove away, past the line of cars belonging to the various Lewis's and away.

CHAPTER TWENTY-ONE
TELL THE TRUTH AND SHAME THE DEVIL

Only a few minutes later, Jazz felt even worse than when she sat in her living room listening to the so-called complete report. She couldn't believe that she'd driven away. Pulling over, Jazz laid her forehead on her steering wheel and sobbed. Big gut-wrenching, runny nose sobs that shook her body. When the sobs subsided, she flipped her sun guard down and looked at herself in the mirror. Aside from the red, watery eyes, the face that stared back at her was the one she'd seen day after day. For a moment, she wished that some physical evidence of the crash could be seen by looking at her. For, even if her body was healed, she still felt bruised. All her injuries were on the inside, and unlike bruises and bone fractures she could cast or ice down, there was no quick cure for her mental wounds. How long would she feel like this? What could she do to speed up the healing?

Maybe she wasn't doing enough. Volunteering at the SibSanc would not be adequate. She had too much free time — too many minutes where she wasn't being useful to society. That was okay when she could kick it with Landi, but now, all her downtime couldn't help her earn God's forgiveness. Clearly, she needed something else, but what?

She sat for a while trying to think of a good project or worthy cause, but nothing came to mind. Finally, she realized that the most immediate thing she could do was be courageous enough to go back home and talk with everyone.

Feeling ashamed that she'd run out like that, Jazz hurried home and felt bad at the immense wave of relief she felt when she saw that all Lewis's cars were gone from in front of her house. She retraced her steps and entered through the kitchen to find her parents seated at the table eating breakfast. A plate of French toast sat waiting for her. Without speaking, Jazz pulled out her chair, plopped down, and began poking at the food on her plate, thinking that it was an amazing gastronomic feat to feel both hungry and nauseous at the same time. She cut a small piece of toast and chewed.

"You okay, kiddo?" asked her father. "That was a little rough, I imagine."

Jazz shrugged. She chewed and swallowed before taking a deep breath and saying, "I knocked it out of her hand."

"Pardon?"

"My cell phone. I knocked it out of Landi's hand."

Both of her parents put down their forks and stared at her. Resisting the urge to look away, Jazz faced them head-on, trying to decipher the looks on their faces.

Deciding the best description would be cautiously curious, she steeled herself and continued.

"She wouldn't tell me what she was texting, so I reached for my phone, and I knocked it out of her hand," confessed Jazz. Saying the words out loud made some of the heaviness that had been weighing down her soul lift some. Before her parents could say or ask anything, Jazz hurried on, "It was my idea to go to the Wash. I, well, I wanted to talk to Brandon, and I knew he'd be there. He'd just broken up with his girlfriend, and I, he. I."

Jazz faltered, embarrassed to have to confess a schoolgirl crush in front of them, but seeing a faint but understanding smile on her mother's face gave her the courage to continue. "So, I convinced Landi to go. She didn't want to, but I told her that Tyrone would be there, so she agreed. Anyway, when we were on our way home, I got a text, and Landi answered it. She told me it was Brandon, but she wouldn't tell me what he was saying. She kept texting and laughing and whatnot. And I was kinda irritated. After a few minutes, I wanted to take a quick peek at the phone, and she tried to get it out of my reach, and I accidentally knocked it out of her hand, and it flew into the back seat. We were laughing. I was annoyed at her, but I was still laughing. Anyway, it buzzed again, and she undid her seatbelt and leaned over the seat to try and reach it. I turned around for a sec to see where the phone was. I thought maybe I could get to it before she could, but it was over behind her seat. I couldn't really see it, so I turned around to see if I could find it. I wasn't looking ahead. I was looking back for my phone, and when I turned back to the road, it was like the elk appeared out of nowhere."

Jazz stopped and grabbed a napkin and wiped her tears away. She took a long breath, swallowed the lump in her throat, and continued, "They were suddenly there in the middle of the road. I don't think I looked away that long. I don't know. Maybe I did. I tried to stop, I really did, but they just stood there, and I didn't want to swerve because of all the trees on either side of the road. I pressed the brake down as hard as I could, but the car kept moving forward. It was like it wasn't even slowing down. I probably should have turned or something. The next thing I know, I hit them and Landi. She sailed backward through the windshield and laid there in the road, not moving. She wasn't moving. Not at all."

Her parents hurried out of their chairs and hugged her. For several long minutes, the three of them held on to each other and sobbed. Finally, when her parents sensed that Jazz had calmed down enough, they released her and returned to their chairs. No one said anything. All three of them wiped their eyes and blew their noses using the napkins at the table.

Jazz looked back and forth from her mother to her father, waiting for one of them to say something. To yell at her, ground her, punish her, do something, but both of her parents seemed at a loss for words. She would have preferred screaming or lecturing. She didn't know what to make of their silence. It made her heart sink.

"Sometimes I don't think I'll ever stop hurting," Jazz said softly, looking down at her plate and pushing the toast from one side of the plate to the other, watching the syrup flow from the space and then slowly seep back into the gap.

"Ever. There will be hours and hours where all I can think about is Landi and how much I miss her. Then, even worse, there will be an hour or so that goes by when she doesn't even come into my head. Those are the worst. The times I feel almost normal. Because then something will happen, usually something small, like a smell, a picture, or something, and it will hit me all over again. I'll remember that I won't be able to tell her what happened in Women's Lit or share a Slurpee big gulp with her. Or have her tell me I need to stop biting my nails. Even going to my stupid locker every day feels like someone is punching me in my stomach. I can't see the end. It feels like all of this will be forever. I'm so sorry sometimes that my entire body hurts."

Jazz looked up and saw the tears coursing down her parents' faces, and the thought occurred to her they were not saying anything because they didn't know what to say. They looked at her with eyes filled to the brim with not only tears but with love, and yet they, too, were at a loss as to how they could help her get through this. Both scared of and relieved by this epiphany, Jazz managed a smile. Who'd have thought that her parents not knowing how to help her would make her feel better—it was nice to know that not having the answers was normal. Jazz cleared her throat, hoping the thick, teary tone she'd been talking with would disappear.

"I guess I will have to keep busy." She hoped her voice sounded more like her formally chipper self. "I think I'll drive by the SibSanc and see if they need me."

"Oh, sweetie," her mother finally said. "It will be alright. I know it doesn't seem like it will now, but it will." She smiled ruefully at Jazz, clearly and fully aware of the lame, useless words she'd uttered. "I'd wish you'd at least finish eating. I think you've lost 10 pounds since the accident."

Jazz nodded. She could tell by the way her clothes fit that she was losing weight. She pulled her plate closer to her and began to methodically eat all the food that sat in front of her. Maybe the toast could help fill the void in her soul that Landi left empty.

An hour later, Jazz sat in the arts and crafts area of the SibSanc, organizing the dozens of cubby holes that held paints, markers, colored pencils, and other craft supplies. The SibSanc was all but empty, and Jazz knew she could easily leave the few kids in the care of mean ole Miss Ruth, but her options, once she left the SibSanc, were all unappealing. Actually, not all of them were unappealing. Shortly after leaving the house and arriving at the hospital, her mother texted her saying that Brandon had called the house phone looking for her. She was thankful that he still thought she didn't have her cell phone. She wasn't up to having the pressure of replying to texts and snaps. Or answering a facetime call. Who would have thought that not having her cell in her hands at all times would be a relief?

While the idea of hanging out with him was appealing, very, very appealing, the idea of her having so much fun, hours after the Lewises had to hear the harrowing details of their daughter's last minutes on earth didn't sit well, seeming way too selfish a thing to do. It was easier to avoid talking with him altogether than telling or texting him no. She tried not to think how pathetic it was that this place designed for little kids was becoming a sanctuary for her. After counting the small number of kids in the place, all of whom were doing a good job of occupying themselves, she again considered going back home. The only thing she could picture herself doing once she got home was crawling into bed, pulling the covers over her head, and doing a little sobbing and sleeping. So instead, Jazz assigned herself the task of re-organizing and cleaning the art corner. She'd been at it a while, a half-hour maybe, content to slave away in the empty room, listening to the Disney music playing, glad that the glass doors were helping her to ignore the pointed, curious looks the older woman gave her from the outer room when out of the corner of her eye she saw Miss Ruth bustling over in her direction, the trademark scowl on her face.

Yanking open the glass doors, the woman stalked over to the table, where Jazz sat working and snapped, "What are you doing here?"

Jazz didn't look up from the half-empty crayon box she was organizing when she answered. "Cleaning up the art corner," she answered, trying with all her might to leach the sarcasm and disrespect she was feeling out of her tone of voice.

Respect your elders, respect your elders, respect the evil, cranky, old elder, the voice in her head chanted.

Maybe dealing with her will satisfy something on your list.

"I can see very well what you're doing," the older woman replied. "I'm asking, what are you doing here? I looked at the check-in sheet. You've been here four times this week. Four. So why are you here, again, on a Saturday afternoon?"

"Our soccer team played Thursday night, our lacrosse team played Friday, and our track team is at a meet in Pueblo," Jazz answered blandly, quite aware that this answer would only irritate the woman. "I've no one to cheer for, so I thought I would use my spare time wisely."

The older woman sighed, clearly exasperated. Jazz turned her head away from Miss Ruth so the woman couldn't see the smirk on her face. Replacing the now rainbow-ordered crayon box, Jazz placidly began sorting the cap-less markers from the capped ones, testing them first out on a scrap piece of paper. For a moment, the only sound was a Disney song playing softly on the overhead speakers, the scrape of dried-out markers on the paper, and Miss Ruth's sighs of annoyance.

"Thank you for your high school sports schedule," the woman said, taking no care at all to hide her sarcasm. "Why are you here? And don't tell me that young man hasn't called you today—seeing as all sporting events have already taken place, and he was mooning over you like a lovesick pup a few days ago."

"He called," admitted Jazz. "So?"

"So, why aren't you on a date with him?"

Jazz shrugged.

"I'm not fluent in sullen teenage body language. You'll have to speak up. Use your words."

"I don't know," muttered Jazz through clenched teeth. "I thought the SibSanc might need some help."

"Hmph. This space was intended to be a sanctuary for those who are healthy."

Jazz stopped her sorting and looked up at the older woman, not bothering to hide her exasperation.

"What's that supposed to mean?"

"The area for those who are hurting is upstairs," the woman answered, her voice suddenly uncharacteristically soft. For the first time, Jazz felt a modicum of warmth and kindness emanating from her.

"I'm fine," declared Jazz, although she'd not been asked how she was.

"Are you?"

Jazz lifted her shoulders again.

Miss Ruth sighed with irritation. "Come here."

Jazz followed the woman to the desk and watched as she pulled out a newspaper clipping. She thrust it at Jazz.

"That about you?"

Jazz looked at the clipping.

Car accident on Route 47 kills one

Last night at 11:40, a Honda Civic ran into a roaming herd of bull elk. Hitting at least one of the animals. The driver, a minor 16 years of age, suffered minor injuries. The passenger, Landi Renee Lewis, died at the scene. While they found no drugs or alcohol at the scene, an investigation into the cause of the accident will occur.

Jazz nodded, "Yes, ma'am." She stared at the clipping, annoyed at the lack of details. Nobody gets it.

"Well?"

"Ma'am?"

"Have you heard when the investigation will be finished?"

"It's finished," Jazz swallowed and blinked, wondering when she could talk about the accident without falling apart. "The police came to my house this morning and gave us their findings."

"And?"

"I wasn't drunk. I wasn't on drugs. I wasn't speeding," Jazz said, hating how defensive she sounded. "I wasn't out past curfew. I wasn't texting or talking on the phone. Those da-, stupid elk were roaming around in the middle of the night, and I hit two. One dead on, and the other I clipped. Landi, she, well, she'd taken off her seatbelt to get a cell phone that had dropped, and she flew through the window when I hit the elk. She died of head and neck injuries."

Jazz said all of this with one breath and felt a little lightheaded. She leaned forward and put her head in her hands, taking large, shuddering breaths as if she'd just finished sobbing. It occurred to her that the elk had suffered the same fate as she and Landi. One had died, while the other one had gone limping off to try and make its way in the world.

"So, it wasn't your fault."

Jazz looked up and snorted derisively. "Of course, it was my fault," she snapped, glaring at the older woman, no longer interested in being respectful. "I was driving. I was reaching for my phone. I wasn't looking at the road. I didn't stop in enough time to avoid hitting the elk!"

"You drove into those elk on purpose?"

"No, of course not, but...."

"You told Landi to take off her seatbelt?"

"No! It's that...."

"It's that you have to take the blame because surely someone is to blame? Because bad luck and accidents don't really happen? Surely it couldn't be bad timing and her God-given time being up? Right? Wait, let me guess. You are here on a beautiful sunny May Saturday afternoon, instead of out with that handsome, polite young man because it isn't fair that Landi can never date, but you can? Is that it? So since the law will not punish you, well then, by God, you'll punish yourself. That sound, about right?"

Jazz looked up at the older woman with amazement. How could this woman, who was at least 65 years old, know what she was thinking and feeling? And so precisely? How could she be the only one who gets it?

As if she'd asked out loud, Miss Ruth answered it, saying, "I understand you because I was you once."

Before she could fix her face into a neutral look, Jazz felt her mouth drop open in disbelief. Was this bitter, mean, short-tempered, caustic woman comparing herself to Jazz? Jazz may not be many things, but self-aware she was. She knew that the words generally used to describe her were charming, bubbly, funny, friendly, and/or silly. Bitter and mean? Surly and sullen? Not even. No way.

Miss Ruth looked at her face and chuckled ruefully. Clearing Jazz's cleaning project away, the woman pulled up a chair and sat down. Jazz waited as the woman gathered her thoughts.

"For most of my life, I was an only child. My daddy left my mom when I was a baby, and for the first 11 years of my life, it was just the two of us. Me and my mom, and that was fine and dandy with me. Then one day, my mother got herself a beau. God, how I hated him," the woman paused and shook her head.

"He was a nice, decent, kind, and generous man, but all I could see was someone who was taking my mom away from me. I was young and immature. Selfish. I gave that poor sainted man such a hard time. They got married anyway. Lord have mercy, I was such a pill at that wedding. I've got such a sour face in every single one of those wedding pictures. Shameful. Don't know why they didn't spank my behind right then and there!"

Miss Ruth grew quiet for a moment, lost in her reverie. She shook her head a bit, and Jazz wondered whether it was a shake of disgust at the memory of herself as an angry only child or a shake to bring herself back to the present. Jazz sat quietly, looking closely at the woman's face, which, lost amid memories, grew softer and younger-looking.

"As I said, they got married,' Miss Ruth continued. "And I got used to having a man around the house. Then I got to liking it. Mom only worked part-time then, and we moved into a little house in Hill Springs, out of our old run-down apartment off Colfax. Life got easy. Nice, comfortable, and even fun. A couple of years into the marriage, my momma got pregnant and had a little boy. Clarence."

"Clarence? You're kidding?" interrupted Jazz. "They named him Clarence? On purpose?"

Miss Ruth gave a sort of snort, and Jazz couldn't tell whether it was in irritation at Jazz for interrupting her or amusement at her reaction to the name.

"Well, it was the 60s. They didn't go around making up names like they do nowadays. As I was saying, they had Clarence. At first, I was okay with it, but then the next thing I knew, I was having to babysit him. He was cute and all, but I was in my teens by then, and cute too. Shapely and pretty. And truth be told, maybe a little fast, I admit, and the last thing I wanted to do with my free time was babysit some little knucklehead baby, even if it was my half-brother. One October weekend, Eugene Jones invites me on the school hayride. And let me tell you, Eugene was all kinds of fine. He put your Brandon to shame...."

"He's not my Brandon!" muttered Jazz.

"Girl, please. Stop being rude. I'm telling a story here."

"Sorry, it's that you keep saying that, Brandon...."

Miss Ruth threw up a hand, cutting Jazz off mid-sentence.

"May I finish?"

Jazz sucked in her breath and resisted the urge to roll her eyes. "Yes, ma'am."

"Thank you. I was about your age, 16, too cute to stand myself, and I'm primping and getting ready for my big date, and Mom comes up, dumps that little squirt on my bed. Says I gotta babysit him 'cause he's catching a cold and she can't take him with her. I am beyond angry. I'd been eyeballin' that Eugene Jones something fierce for months, and he finally broke up with this fast tail girl he'd been seeing and asks me out, and now I'm gonna have to cancel? I was too hot, but we did as we were told back then. Not like your poorly behaved generation."

"So, there I am, mad as all get out, and that Clarence is fussing and sick, and not his usual happy self, which made it even worse. We were both miserable, I can tell you that. Finally, he goes down for his afternoon nap, and I stomp my angry self outside and sit on my front porch fuming and thinking about how I have the worst life in the whole world. Well, who drives up in a smokin' black mustang? Nobody but Eugene. Girl, I 'bout fell over. All I could think of was that I was glad I hadn't changed out of my cute outfit. And I'm all fluttery and happy 'cause he didn't go and ask some other girl to go on the hayride with him, and suddenly I have the best life in the whole wide world, 'cause here he is, at my house! Lawd, have mercy. I could have died of happiness right there! He walks his fine ole self up to my porch, and we start to talking and laughing. And one thing leads to another, and we start necking."

Jazz's eyebrows shot up at this revelation, and Ms. Ruth rolled her eyes. "Child, please, don't think ya'll the ones who made up kissing. Kissing been around since before Moses. Besides, I told you I was a little fast."

Jazz can't help but give the woman a smile. As Ms. Ruth was telling the story, Jazz could clearly see the shadows of the young, pretty teenager smitten with a handsome boy playing across the woman's visage. It made her think differently about the usually unpleasant lady.

"Go, on Miss Ruth. I'm listening."

"Good, because here comes the vital part of this whole story. I'm canoodling with my beau and feeling fine and dandy. And we are at each other for a good bit. Finally, we come up for air, and I glance at my watch, 'cause the last thing I needed was for my momma and daddy to come driving up while I'm making out with some boy — I started calling him daddy, soon as my nose was no longer out of joint about him loving my mama too. Well, it's been a good long while since Clarence went down for his nap, and I hadn't even peeked in at him. A good long while. Now, that Clarence was a pretty easy baby. Happy, cute, and kept to his schedule like clockwork. Down for a nap after lunch, sleep for an hour and a half, maybe two, then back up. Well, according to my watch, it was going on two and a half, almost dang near three hours since I put him down. I knew he was coming down with a bug, but I didn't know whether that meant he was gonna sleep longer or what. I mean, I was a kid. Despite that, I hadn't given him any medicine. Momma did, before she left, but I knew that three hours was too long for Clarence to be asleep. If I hadn't been kissing on that boy, I would have checked on him way earlier. I know I would have, 'cause I enjoyed watching him sleep. It was calming. He was such a cute little baby. I'm thinking I better go see about him. I run into the kitchen, grab Eugene a soda, and then skip my happy behind upstairs to see what is happening with Clarence. Like I said, he was a happy baby. I kind of figured he was up in his crib, cooing and playing. He wouldn't do too much screaming unless he was messy or hungry. I wasn't even all that worried, just kind of curious, you know. So, I quietly open the door to his nursery and, I look down into the crib, and, and…."

Her story stopped abruptly as Miss Ruth choked up. Getting up from the table, she snatched a tissue from the boxes that are stuck strategically around the SibSanc in case of a breakdown. She blew her nose and dabbed her eyes, her back partially turned away from Jazz.

"I haven't talked about this in years. It must be going on fifty years since I even said his name to another soul," whispered Miss Ruth, as if more to herself than to Jazz. She wiped her eyes again, her lips tightened, and Jazz could see both the scared young girl and the sad older woman on her face at the same time.

After a last blow, Miss Ruth took a deep breath and said softly, "He must have been coming down with the flu because there was vomit everywhere in the crib. And when I picked him up, he was limp. He wasn't breathing or anything. When I held him up, there was vomit leaking out of his mouth, his nose, but there was nothing else on that little boy that was moving. Everything about him was still, except that throw-up dripping out of him, and I knew instantly I was holding a shell. Our little Clarence was gone. I must have screamed bloody murder because Eugene comes bursting into the room. Even after all these years, I don't remember too much after that. I remember hearing piercing screams, almost as if they were coming from a distance. I knew they were coming from me, but it wasn't as if I could stop myself. Then I guess something in me broke."

Miss Ruth grabbed another tissue and blew her nose before handing a clean one to Jazz, who had to dry her eyes as well.

"Nobody blamed me," continued Miss Ruth in a voice that sounded years younger than she looked. "He could have vomited a minute after I laid him down or two hours after. Aspirated the stuff into his lungs, they said. Drowned on it. Things were a little different back then. No investigation that I know of. No report on the internet, of course, didn't exist back then. Just a short little obituary in the paper, a program at the funeral. That's all the reporting that was made on the event that altered my life so drastically. My parents bought a tiny white coffin. I tried my best not to look at that white coffin for the whole service. I kept my eyes on my shoes while my mom and stepdad buried their little son. I faded away while they somehow struggled and got back to life. They treated me as lovingly as ever, maybe even more so, but I couldn't get over the fact that I hadn't gone up to check on him at all. Not once. If only I had, I might have gotten there in time. Been able to hold him upright while he vomited. Cleaned it out of his mouth, made sure he could breathe when he was through throwing up. If I had been a more attentive babysitter, Clarence wouldn't have died. I still think that, after all these years. Think about how I should have thanked Eugene politely for coming and made another date with him at a more appropriate time. Should have gotten a book and read in the rocking chair in Clarence's room until he woke up. Or stayed inside and watched television and checked on him during each commercial break. That's all I could think about, the 'what ifs' and the 'if onlys' and the 'should'ves,' I was obsessed with all the possibilities, with what actions I could have chosen that would have kept my baby brother alive."

Miss Ruth's voice petered out, and Jazz could see in her eyes that those same fifty-year-old thoughts were still playing on an endless loop in her head. An intense wave of sadness washed over her, and it was almost refreshing because, for the first time in weeks, her sorrow was for someone else's grief and sadness rather than her own. There was some relief in feeling for a person beside herself or Landi. She had to repress an urge to hug the old woman, knowing instinctively that Miss Ruth would not accept any solace, although Jazz didn't know whether it would be a hug of thanks for the woman reaching out to her or a hug to provide the woman with comfort. Instead, she reached over and gently squeezed the old woman's hand. Miss Ruth looked startled at the touch and slid her hand away, clutching it with her other hand and holding it in her lap in such a way that Jazz thought it was to keep herself from reaching back to grab Jazz's still outstretched hand. Jazz watched as the old woman's lips thinned, her eyes grew narrower, almost as if she was closing herself off again. Shutting down the soft, vulnerable parts of her soul, she'd briefly exposed for Jazz's benefit. The woman drew a deep breath, almost as if continuing to talk took tremendous physical effort.

After a beat, Miss Ruth refocused her attention and stared intensely into Jazz's eyes, as if everything she'd just said paled in importance to what she was about to say.

"Jazz, I didn't feel right having any fun after Clarence passed. I'd feel bad if I laughed or smiled. My guilt was physically painful if I realized I was having fun. The realization that I was on the verge of feeling happy would make me sick to my stomach. So eventually, I stopped going out. Stopped everything that remotely resembled fun. Told that fine Eugene Jones to leave me alone and never darken my doorstep again. Pushed him away with two hands."

Miss Ruth paused again, gazed at a spot above Jazz's head as if looking at a screen that showed her past, and said wistfully, "He grew up to be a good man, good father last I heard. Nice job, happy family, treats his wife like a queen...."

The old woman's eyes took on a faraway, yearning look, and she fell silent again. Jazz watched as her eyes returned to the present and became stern again.

"Anyway," she continued, her voice growing tight and curt. "I knew Clarence's death was my fault, and I was dead certain that I didn't deserve any sort of happiness. And I made sure I didn't get any. I stopped wearing cute clothes and dressed like a widow for the rest of high school and even throughout college. I was mean and nasty to my friends and eventually drove away every friend and acquaintance I had. I was cold and distant to my parents, even though I could see I was breaking their hearts all over again. I realize now, looking back, they lost two children, not one, that day. I was never mentally present in my life after that afternoon. I turned into a passive, uninvolved observer, and a mean one at that."

"Pretty soon, it was a habit, having a negative, unfriendly attitude. Years pass so quickly, I know it don't seem like that to you now, but they do. One day you're 16, then the next, you're 61. Seems like a blink of an eye sometimes. But next thing I knew, I was alone and bitter and ill-tempered. An unmarried, unloved 67-year-old woman who is steadily getting older. I've got more life behind me now than I do in front of me. Thought I should do something about trying to get into heaven. Figured I'd do some volunteering. See if I can earn my way in there before it's too late. But even now, 50 years later, I feel the guilt of his death. I wear it like a coat now. It's thick and heavy but strangely comfortable. Familiar, I guess. Old people don't like to change. To be honest with you, I'm pretty sure that this little bit of hospital charitable work will not be enough to cast off the guilt. Don't even know if I want to be without it; after 50 years, it's all I know. It's been the one constant in my life."

Miss Ruth fell silent, and Jazz watched as the shadow of the happy young teen on her face faded away completely, the customary scowl and frown lines embedded in the woman's face reappearing. They looked deep and permanent.

"I'm no fool, Jazz. I know how terse and unpleasant I am—especially compared to the sweetness and light of Miss Daisy Brooks. We're diametric opposites, the two of us. She's love and warmth; I'm anger and coldness. I know why I've been shunted from one department here in the hospital to another. People don't enjoy being around me. Can't say as I blame them either. I devoted my life to my guilt until it turned into bitterness. I made it a point never to forgive myself. I've traveled that road, and I can see you making baby steps in that same direction. I'm telling you to stop. I'm telling you to forgive yourself. I'm telling you that you'll never know why Landi died, and you didn't. But you have to learn to live again, without her, and without that guilt. You have to, Jazz, or you'll end up like me."

CHAPTER TWENTY-TWO
WAKE THE DEAD

Long after Jazz was home and in bed, the words and the story that Miss Ruth had told her reverberated in her mind, like a refrain from a song that you couldn't get out of your head. Her warning scared Jazz in a few different ways. She was now frightened that she wouldn't be able to live again, not without Landi by her side. Afraid that she didn't have the courage to move on by herself without the support of her best friend, and more than anything, startled by the realization that she found it easier, in some ways, to collapse inward, as if she was a little roly-poly bug, than it would be to force herself back outward, back into the life that she knew was waiting for her.

Jazz was also terrified that maybe it was too late for her to change her path. Maybe she'd already taken too many steps in the wrong direction like Miss Ruth had said. Perhaps happiness and normal were too far behind her now for her to regain them. Already she was getting more and more comfortable being by herself — used to being on the peripheral of life, watching rather than participating, listening rather than talking. She could never be the Jazz Sanders she was, so who would she be? And more importantly, could she ever do enough to earn her way into heaven, or would she be like Miss Ruth, in the twilight of her life, being shunted from department to department, still trying to earn her way in?

She fell asleep that night without figuring out an answer to a single one of those questions.

•   •

Another week went by. Then another.

Another week without Landi, and while her classmates all moved on to other things, Jazz continued to struggle. Each day, she was still mentally exhausted from pretending to be her old self. The only solace she got was the time she spent helping at the Sib Sanc. She got good at ignoring the pointed, knowing looks from Ms. Ruth, and luxuriated in the warmth and kindness that was Grandma Daisy. Another week of trying to avoid Brandon without appearing to avoid him. She answered his texts, doing everything she could to shuttle him off into the Friendzone. Even on those days, they both appeared at the Sib Sanc at the same time. She studiously tried to avoid working together with him, even as Ms. Ruth kept trying to assign them the same tasks.

Even so, it was not enough. No matter what she filled her time with, cheering, homework, volunteering, it still felt like she how hours and hours still left on her hands to think. She needed more stuff to do. More ways to earn points in the game of forgiveness.

The third Sunday morning of May, Jazz attended church, again, with her astonished parents. And frankly, their reaction was getting insulting. After all, she'd been to church for at least four weeks in a row, so why the surprised looks each Sunday morning? Seriously. It was so disrespectful.

After service, while her parents took advantage of the balmy spring day and go play a little golf, Jazz drove around aimlessly. It wasn't so much aimless, as it was cowardly, because there was a definite someplace she needed to go, but she was having a very hard time steering her car in that direction. While at church, some hidden force, her best friend's ghost probably, had forced her arm up when a volunteer was needed to replace Landi as the vice-chair of the young adult group. Frankly, after seeing the amazed faces of her peers in the youth group, she'd almost told them to forget it, but she ignored the looks of bewilderment and rose above their shock and pettiness, although it hadn't been easy. Her first impulse was to blow the whole thing off, but she was determined to earn more points into heaven, and what better way than to work in one of his houses? That had to be worth bonus points. Unfortunately, taking over for Landi meant that someone needed to gather the folder and other random church stuff from the Lewises, and Jazz (or Landi's spirit?) volunteered, again. After all, it made little sense for someone else to get it since it was stuff she was going to need.

Gathering her courage, she got into her car after church and went straight to... the coffee house. It was warm, and an iced vanilla latte would be nice. Then, right after she grabbed the latte, she headed directly... home. She needed to change her shoes, 'cause her feet hurt in those heels. Then she... wandered through the house and thought it would be nice to help, so she cleaned the kitchen, did a load of laundry, vacuumed the family room.

Then she spent a good hour simply looking at her phone. Tracing the cracks on her screen. After her trip to the SibSanc the day of the officer's report, she'd gone to her room to find it sitting on her desk. Charging. It was at 47%, but that day she unplugged it and silenced it, and threw it in her drawer.

Out of sight. Out of mind.

Except for the buzzing that occurred fairly frequently. Muffled but loud enough to be heard through the closed drawer.

Unable to resist the temptation, she pulled open the again drawer and peeked at her phone, found her charger, and plugged it in. Then, before she knew it, she was looking at Instagram. Carefully avoiding the pages of her classmates, she scrolled through the pages of her favorite celebrities before becoming bored. How she had wasted hours doing that before the crash, she didn't know. She reopened the drawer and was about to toss the phone back in when Ruth and her story popped unbidden into her head. Sighing, she held the phone in her hand, marveling that her first instinct was not to tuck it into her back pocket or open it up and scroll but to get it as far away from her as possible.

The woman's voice drifted into her head.

"You have to learn to live again."

Closing her eyes, she fingered the cracked screen again. Her phone was cracked but still worked and was usable.

Just like me. Still usable.

Tossing the phone back, she shut the drawer with a bang and bolted from the room before the phone pulled her back. She returned to the laundry room and moved the clothes from the washer to the dryer. Then stood in the kitchen looking for something to do.

Finally, having run out of things to do, she'd walked slowly to her car. She stood with her hand on the door. As if by some magical force, she spun around, ran up the stairs, and grabbed her phone, sliding into her back pocket.

After taking the most circuitous route possible, she mentally gathered all her courage and drove down their street, pulled into the Lewis's driveway, and shut off her car. And sat there, scared to get out and fervently wishing that Landi would come sauntering out of the house.

She squeezed her eyes shut, feeling the courage she used to drive over trickle away. There was too much fear in her and not nearly enough nerve to open the door. She could always ring the bell again rather than waltz right in as Mrs. Lewis said she should, but what if it was Linny who answered the door again? How would he react to seeing her? And what would she say to him? She didn't think she could survive another confrontation like the one the last time she was at the Lewis's house. That thought was enough to make Jazz realize that she did not have enough guts to even get out of her car, much less ring their doorbell. She put her head on the steering wheel and searched her soul for the bravery needed to get out of her car and walk to the front door and face whoever answered it.

Finding none, she gave a shuddering sigh and reached her hand towards the ignition. There was no reason to get that stuff today. There were at least six more days before it would be needed. Her eyes still squeezed shut to keep the tears abated. She fumbled around, searching for the key, and was about to turn on the ignition when a tap on the window made her jump. Opening her eyes, she saw Mr. Lewis peering through the window.

He beckoned her out and took a step back so she could open her car door. She emerged from the car with shaky legs and an even shakier smile.

"Hey there, Little Miss One Note, you okay?"

Jazz smiled despite her intense feelings of fear, sadness, and longing. Little Miss One Note.

Only Mr. Lewis called her that. Like his daughter, he loved doling out nicknames. Jazz had always been a least a head shorter than Landi, and Mr. Lewis called her One Note because she was a "short little toot."

"Hi DaddyTooTwo," she said softly.

He pulled her into a big bear hug.

"You doing okay?"

Jazz smiled up at him and shrugged, "Fair to middling."

Mr. Lewis laughed. "Watch it now. You can't be stealing my lines. You young people always biting off us! Ya'll better get your own material!"

"That's 'cause you old people have all the best stuff."

"You got that right, and who you calling old?"

"I would never call you old, Mr. Lewis. Mature maybe, or properly aged. Like wine."

"What you know about wine, little girl?"

"Um, that's it—old, old grape juice?"

Mr. Lewis laughed, "Whew, I sure do miss you and that mouth of yours. You looking for Melinda?"

"Not really. I was here to pick up the YPD stuff because I'm replacing Lan...." Jazz trailed off. Mr. Lewis's face immediately lost some of the joviality that had appeared doing their earlier chatter at her words. A moment passed, and Mr. Lewis recovered and gave her a quick smile.

"I'm going to be the vice-chair for the YPD at church," Jazz finished, pretending the awkward pause never occurred. "I, we, need the notes and folders and stuff."

Mr. Lewis patted Jazz on the shoulder. "Good for you. Glad you are going to church on a regular basis instead of pretending to be asleep."

Jazz's mouth dropped open. "Wha-, how did, I mean, what are you talking about? I was tired those mornings. I'm very busy. I'm growing. I need my rest. I have no idea what you are trying to imply."

"Girl, please, my generation invented playing possum on Sunday mornings!" Mr. Lewis burst out laughing, "Didn't I say that your generation steals all our best stuff?"

Jazz laughed. She had always loved talking with Mr. Lewis.

After gathering the church things, Mr. Lewis walked Jazz to the doorway, "I'll tell Melinda you stopped by. I know she's told you this, but I want to say it, too. We miss you. Please come by and say hi to a couple of old people whenever you get a chance."

Jazz wrapped her arms around the man who was like another father to her and squeezed. "I will. I promise DaddyTooTwo."

Mr. Lewis hugged her back and laid his cheek on the top of her head for a second. Then abruptly, he took her by the shoulders and said to her sternly, staring into her eyes, "I loved my daughter with all my heart. But she wasn't perfect. Well, she was a perfect daughter, but not a perfect person. Nobody is, of course. You know as well as I do that some of those nicknames she gave out were downright mean. Funny, maybe, and usually with a kernel of truth to 'em but mean all the same. She was a bossy thing, too. I didn't always like the way she could boss you around. Of course, that comes from her momma's side. Judgmental, a bit inflexible at times. Oh, and a bit of a snob, too. She gets that from Melinda's people, too, in case you were wondering. She was wonderful. Flawed, spoiled, occasionally attitudinal, but so incredible. Her being gone is like having a chunk of my heart missing. It's a constant ache, but she was not a saint. Sometimes when the people we love pass, we get to thinking about how wonderful they were and forget that they had faults, just like the rest of us. Can't tell you how many funerals I've been to where the pastor's up there talking about how so-and-so's in heaven. All the while, I'm thinking, 'I wouldn't be so sure that so-and-so will be making it into heaven if I was you, Reverend.' My point is, Jazz, remember Landi as she was. Don't remake your memories of her into some saintly, never do wrong girl. Honor her by remembering her exactly as she was, not a cleaned-up, sanitized version of your best friend. And, this part is real important. One Note, don't go trying to replace Landi. I mean, if you like volunteering at the hospital, then keep doing it. If you don't, then stop. If you want to be the co-chair of them hard-headed young uns at church, fine. But don't do it because that is what Landi did. We've lost my Landi. We don't want to lose our Jazz too. Got it? Oh Lord, look what I've done. Here, use my hanky."

Jazz sniffed noisily and only dabbed her eyes with his cotton handkerchief, not wanting to hand him back a snotty one.

"Thank you, DaddyTooTwo," Jazz said. "Thank you."

"You're welcome, One Note, don't be a stranger."

Jazz hurried to her car to get a tissue to wipe her dripping nose. Giving Mr. Lewis a last hug, she stood for a moment, wiping her eyes.

As she headed down the steps, a car pulled into the driveway. Instantly her blood pressure shot up as the heart started being triple time.

Linny.

For one panicked moment, she almost turned around and hurried back into the house. Luckily, she stopped herself. The last thing Linny would want was her seeking protection from his parents.

Even with the look of anger on his face, she automatically thought about how handsome he was. She couldn't help it. The sticky ties of her girlhood crush still ensnared her, which made the first words out of his mouth even that much more painful.

"Why can't you leave my family alone? Haven't you done enough?"

Jazz vaguely gestured to the church stuff in her hand, "No, I mean yes. It's, I, the YPD stuff."

Linny gave a cursory glance at the notebooks and snorted. "First the SibSanc and now the YPD? So damn fake. You will never replace Landi. Ever. You're like the Farrah Franklin to Landi's Beyoncé."

That comment threw Jazz so much that she responded to him as if he still was her friend for a moment. "Um, Farrah? Who's that Lin?"

"Exactly. Without Landi, you are forgettable. Like the disregarded member of Destiny's Child. The person people don't care enough about to even remember they exist. In the interest of keeping it real? Fact is that I don't care what the police report says. I don't care about what my parents say, and most of all, I don't care about you. All that forgiveness everyone is preaching is bullshit. Because of you, I don't have a little sister. Because of you, one of my favorite people no longer exists. Because of you, my mom's only daughter is gone. Because of you. You know what? The rest of my family can go around acting like they are in some damn Hallmark/Disney movie. They can quote scriptures and talk about moving on and about forgiveness and about how you are just like family and all that other bullshit. But as Arya Stark says, that ain't me. I will always blame you for this. Always."

And with that, Linny brushed by her, opened the door, and closed it with a finality that sent her fleeing to her car, tears streaming down her face.

Driving recklessly, Jazz hurriedly put as much distance between her and what had just happened as she could. All that was waiting for her at home were a couple of chapters of English lit reading and a physics worksheet. Not to mention the fact that she knew she looked like she'd been sobbing. She pulled over, flipped the sun protector down, and looked in the mirror. Sure enough, her eyes were red and swollen, her nose dripping. If she walked into the house like this, there'd be questions, and she didn't want to lie or withhold information from her parents again, not after holding on to such a big secret for so long. No, if asked what happened, she'd tell the truth. The truth could lead to a phone call to the Lewis'. Which would lead to the Lewis' confronting Linny. Could they force him to forgive her? Would that really be true forgiveness if they did? Even though what Linny said hurt her, he got to feel the way he wanted. Mr. Lewis and Mrs. Lewis willingly forgave her, and that was their choice. But no one could dictate how long Linny would stay anger. No one could tell him how to grieve. No one could demand he feel something for Jazz that he didn't truly feel. Life wasn't a Disney movie. Struggles and problems didn't always get solved with a happily ever after ending. The girl didn't always kiss the right boy at the end.

She would have to give up her childish fantasies of ending up with him. She would have to be okay with him not forgiving her. His choice gave her no choice.

Still in no shape to head home, Jazz found herself, instead, walking into the narthex of the Catholic church. The silence of the church soothed her. It was also nice to think that she could sit here and think without running into anyone she knew. Somewhere she could sit and wait for her eyes to go back to normal without a thousand questions.

Sitting on the padded bench, Jazz heaved a sigh and looked at the stained glass windows, enjoying the way the light made some of them glow bright while casting colorful shadows on the opposing wall.

"Jazz?"

Looking behind her, she saw Father Peter in an elaborate vestment walking towards her. She stood, wondering if perhaps the church was closed or something. He waved her back down with a smile.

"Hey there, Father Peter. How was service today?"

"Mass was lovely. Thanks for asking. You should join us sometime. Are you okay?"

Jazz nodded. "It's quiet here. Peaceful. Soothing."

Father Peter sat in the pew directly in front of Jazz and nodded. "It is."

They sat silently for a moment.

"Hey. I gotta question for you," Jazz said suddenly, her voice seeming too loud in the quiet chapel. She lowered her voice to a whisper, "You know that whole absolution stuff?"

Father Peter whispered back, "Yes. It's not a secret. We all know about it. You don't have to whisper. Mass has been over for about three hours."

Jazz gave him a quick smile before beginning again seriously, "What does it mean to 'ransom the captive'? I mean, does it really mean to pay money to kidnappers?"

Father Peter frowned. "I'm sorry? What?"

"Well, one of the acts of mercy is to 'ransom the captive,' and I was wondering if you could give me a better explanation than Wikipedia."

"Oh, Lord." Father Peter shook his head and chuckled to himself.

"What? It's a valid question."

"Acts of Mercy? You looked up Acts of Mercy and got your answer from Wikipedia?"

"Hey, Wikipedia has everything, dude, er Father!"

"And what did it say?"

"Well, it said to visit prisoners. I don't know any, so I was wondering if I could maybe skip that one, especially if that's what it means, and maybe feed people twice or donate more clothes."

Father Peter looked at her for a moment before scratching his head.

"You know Jazz, I've been thinking a lot about your situation, and I think that all the Good Lord wants from you is that you try your best every day to be a good person. He doesn't expect us to be perfect. Only his son was perfect. I think that as long as you are kind and generous and loving, your chances are no better or worse than anyone else's in terms of getting into heaven. Accident or no accident. So, what it means is to show mercy to those who are imprisoned or oppressed somehow. It's a corporal act of mercy, but now that I think about it, for you, it could be more of a spiritual act."

Jazz sighed, feeling surprisingly relieved because, for the first time in weeks, her reaction to words like the ones that Father Peter said weren't ones of absolute disbelief and self-hatred. She felt, if not completely healed, then at least healing. Not knowing what to say, Jazz sat silently, enjoying feeling a little lighter than she had for weeks and weeks.

"What I mean to say, in common English, Jazz," continued Father Peter after a moment. "Maybe the prisoner you need to free is yourself. Maybe the one to who you need to show mercy is sitting right here. You need to free yourself from the mental prison you've locked yourself in."

Those simple words opened a flood gate, and Jazz fumbled in her purse for a tissue to dry the onslaught of tears that were coursing down her cheeks.

"I don't know you very well, but from our few encounters, I can tell that you are trying to keep yourself caged. Not your physical self, but your soul. It's as if there is a beautiful bird that is used to singing and flying free, and you are trying to keep all that beauty and freedom locked up as some sort of tribute to your friend. Or perhaps, as a punishment to yourself. I don't confess to know why the Lord does what he does but think I can safely say that he doesn't take someone away to somehow punish someone else."

Jazz nodded.

"Look, what would your friend... What was her name?"

"Landi."

"What would Landi be telling you to do? What would she say if she were here right now?"

Closing her eyes, Jazz dove into her well of memories. She let it wash over her and surprised herself by giving a snort with repressed laughter. Opening her eyes, she looked into the priest's curious face and said, smiling through her tears, "Landi would say, 'Ugh, I'm so over you, and you're "my best friend is dead angst." Can you move on? Honestly, Jazz, you can be so overdramatic. Enough already. All this whining isn't doing anything but annoying me! Get over it already, geez.'"

Then Mr. Lewis's words popped into her head. Jazz managed to grin at Father Peter, adding, "And to be perfectly honest, if we were out of earshot of any adults, she would have sprinkled in a whole bunch of bad words, using the worst ones as nouns, verbs, adjectives, and adverbs. Landi could curse like a sailor." Jazz smiled to herself, enjoying talking about her friend. Not the martyred, saintly version she'd been creating in her head the last few weeks, but the real-life flawed one. The wonderful girl who'd been by her side most of her life. She fell silent as she tried to figure out what Landi would be saying to Linny. She honestly didn't know, and a small lump formed in her throat.

The ache of grief was still there, but it wasn't as sharp. The lump not so large that she couldn't swallow it down and continue to speak.

"She had this innocent face, but her mouth was awful. I blame her brothers." Jazz grabbed her phone and showed the priest the picture she used as her home screen of her and Landi.

Father Charles chuckled. "She does look quite sweet, doesn't she? Well, now the question you need to ask yourself is whether you will ransom yourself? Will you take the advice that your best friend would have given you if she could?"

Jazz opened her mouth but had no real answer for the priest. Could she forgive herself? She knew for certain that Landi would want her to start living again. "Oh my God, Jazz," she would have said, her face pinched with irritation. "Get fucking over yourself."

Could she get over herself so she could forgive herself? Jazz didn't know.

"Oh, for fuck's sake, Jazz, move on already!"

Landi's voice was so crystal clear in her head that the next thing she knew, she was pulling her phone out of her pocket. She scrolled quickly, listening with pleasure to the click of her fingernails on her phone for the first time in weeks. Then, taking a deep breath, she pressed send. Maybe she could move on, maybe she couldn't. The only thing she knew was that she now felt like she could start trying.

She and Father Peter sat in silence for a moment. She thanked him and left the church, her mind buzzing in a way it hadn't since the accident. So many adult voices in her head. Daddy TooTwo, Father Peter's. Miss Ruth's. Whenever she had too much on her mind, she had always had Landi to go to. For a while, she drove aimlessly, grabbing a Frappuccino that sat in her drink holder sweating. She needed someone who could listen to her, then help her sort through the maze of her thoughts. And she knew who it was.

CHAPTER TWENTY-THREE
RANSOMING THE CAPTIVE

Parking in the cemetery lot, Jazz walked over to Landi's grave. Now that it was late spring, the Crabapple trees near Landi's plot were in full bloom. Landi had loved this time of year. She had loved when the blossoms on the trees were out. If not for the rows of gravestones, the cemetery would have looked like a park. Someone had been to visit her grave recently because there were some relatively fresh flowers in the smallholder attached to her headstone.

Jazz kneeled beside the plot and traced the letters with her fingers. Forever cherished.

"Hey," she whispered. She held her breath for a moment and waited. Nothing. No voice from beyond. No sudden feeling of calm or warmth. She sighed, feeling disappointed. People always seemed to be comforted by talking to their loved ones in the cemetery in the movies. They also appeared to chat so easily with them. Jazz wanted to pour her heart out, but she didn't feel comforted. Talking to Landi didn't come easy because Jazz just didn't feel like Landi was there, somehow, beneath her.

"I miss you. So much," she whispered it more to herself than to the grave. Wishing there was some way for her to know that Landi heard her. "I'm so sorry."

A breeze suddenly blew, creating a swirl of pink petals from the flowering trees to dance in the air. Looking up, she watched as the air spun the petals around her, encircling her. Landi had loved that too, that the trees' flowers would burst out, create sudden beauty, and then drop from the trees just as quickly. "Transitory beauty," she had called it once. Jazz had rolled her eyes and replied, "Nice use of one of this week's vocabulary words."

Sighing, she stuffed her hands in her pockets. It was Landi's favorite time of day. The golden hour. If they were ever together when the Golden Hour hit, everything had to stop while they took selfies. "The light is perfect. Our melanin be poppin' in this light." Landi would announce, and they would huddle close together and snap dozens of pictures and spend ten minutes arguing which one to post. She pulled out her phone, but there was no one to take a photo with, so she shoved it back in her jacket, noticing for the first time that there was a little piece of paper in her pocket, which she pulled out. A fortune from a fortune cookie. It must have been sitting in her pocket for at least a year. It'd been a while since she'd had this jacket on.

Happiness is a choice.

Not really a fortune. Which was exactly what she had gripped to Landi after reading it. Landi had shrugged and said, "No. But it's facts, though, right? Like, when shit happens, you can choose to focus on the shit. Like really focus on whining and wallowing in the shittiness of the shit. Or, you can also choose to focus on the fact that shit is like fertilizer and make stuff grow. So, you can choose to wallow or choose to grow."

Choose to wallow.

Or choose to grow.

Wiping the tears that had been rolling down her cheeks, Jazz looked down and saw that a single perfect, heart-shaped petal had landed on her lap. Picking it up, she lifted it on one finger, holding it up to the perfect light of Golden Hour. Grabbing her phone, she took a picture of it there, perched on her finger, its pink glowing against the light of the setting sun. It sat on her finger for a moment before another warm breeze lifted up and carried it away.

Wallow or grow.

The stillness of the cemetery was suddenly broken by an electronic ding from her back pocket. Her phone.

Hey there Got ur text I see u got your phone back You there? Wanna hang out?

Happiness is a choice.

When life gives you shit - Choose to wallow or choose to grow.

Maybe Landi was talking to her all along.

Choose to grow.

Jazz took a deep breath and stared at the phone cradled in her hand and made a choice.

She texted back.

`Yep, but first meet me at the Sib Sanc.`

...The Beginning

About the Author

Traci L. Jones holds a B.A. in psychology from Pomona College in Claremont, CA. An M.A. in advertising from the University of Denver, and has taken several courses in Creative Writing at the University of Denver.

Before launching a young adult novelist career, Traci L. Jones wrote articles for the local business magazines, *In The Black and Emerging Markets.*

Traci L. Jones' first YA novel, *Standing Against the Wind,* was published in 2006 with Farrar, Straus, and Giroux (FSG), and won the Coretta Scott King/John Steptoe New Talent Award. Her second novel, *Finding My Place* also published by FSG in 2010. Her third novel, *Silhouetted by the Blue* (FSG), was released in July 2011 and received a starred review from Booklist.

Note from the Author

Word-of-mouth is crucial for any author to succeed. If you enjoyed *Ransoming the Captive*, please leave a review online — anywhere you are able. Even if it's just a sentence or two. It would make all the difference and would be very much appreciated.

Thanks!
Traci L. Jones

We hope you enjoyed reading this title from:

www.blackrosewriting.com

Subscribe to our mailing list – *The Rosevine* – and receive **FREE** books, daily deals, and stay current with news about upcoming releases and our hottest authors.
Scan the QR code below to sign up.

Already a subscriber? Please accept a sincere thank you for being a fan of Black Rose Writing authors.

View other Black Rose Writing titles at
www.blackrosewriting.com/books and use promo code
PRINT to receive a **20% discount** when purchasing.
hasing.